Rina

THE DONOR
The Michael Duffy Story

Eustelle Harvey

MINERVA PRESS
ATLANTA LONDON SYDNEY

THE DONOR: *The Michael Duffy Story*
Copyright © Eustelle Harvey 1999

ISBN 0 75410 674 8

First Published 1999 by
MINERVA PRESS
315–317 Regent Street
London W1R 7YB

Printed in Great Britain for Minerva Press

THE DONOR
The Michael Duffy Story

Eustelle Harvey was born in Dublin. She trained as a nurse in a London hospital during the war, married a doctor who became a surgeon and they moved to Londonderry, Northern Ireland. They have three daughters and four grandchildren and over the years they have been very involved in all aspects of Red Cross work and many other charities. Eustelle has been a member of the Board of Visitors at HM Prison Magilligan for almost twenty years. In 1987 she was awarded the MBE and in 1991 she was appointed High Sheriff of Londonderry, the first woman to hold that office in that city.

Extract from foreword of *Red Cross Recall* by Eustelle Harvey, published by Blackthorn Group in 1991.

Acknowledgements

To Ailish Gallagher, OBE, Former Assistant Director of the Western Health and Social Board of Northern Ireland.

To Mrs A. Ferris, who has typed this MS so beautifully.

To Ronald, my husband, who has always supported me while working on this book, with all my love.

Part One

Prologue

Elsie never knew why she married Tom. She always said
that marriage was not for her, that it was a trap in which
women were caught. Love and romance soon wore very
thin and were replaced by years of child rearing, skimping
and slaving to make ends meet. She had seen her mother
and aunts becoming old women before they were forty. All
right for some but not for her; she had always wanted to be
free to come and go just as she pleased and not to be tied to
one bedroom and to one man. Elsie needed space to
breathe and to be herself, which was why she left home and
set herself up in a bedsit in the city and well away from the
family. She had worked in various jobs and she liked to
change from one kind of work to another to avoid
becoming bored. She had worked in a home bakery, in
Woolworths and also in a shirt factory.

Tom Draper was twenty years older than Elsie, who had
come to housekeep for him when he was recovering from
pneumonia. She was capable and cheerful; she had taken
over the house and had nursed Tom back to health. Tom
had realised that he had not been so well looked after since
his wife had died ten years ago. The local women who had
come to clean the house, do some shopping, wash his
clothes and prepare his midday meal had in no way
provided the care Elsie had given him.

Elsie was not unattractive, in her own way. She had
bright blue eyes and a blooming complexion. Although
beginning to put on fat, there was something about her that

Tom found pleasing as he watched her go about the house in a most competent manner. Tom considered asking her to marry him, more so that she could continue to undertake the management of his house than to become his bedfellow. He was too old and busy to form any deep attachments.

A pity to let a good housekeeper go. I can't keep a woman in the house now that I am well, he thought, especially a woman like Elsie.

Elsie became quite fond of Tom, as he was quiet and undemanding, but she was in no way in love with him. She loved the solid old farmhouse with its large kitchen, warmed by the Aga cooker, a real joy to cook on, and she loved the series of pantries and sculleries where there was room for everything: the washing on wet days, the Wellington boots and walking sticks and room to spare, so unlike her home where there was never room for anything and where to find a required article meant moving any number of things.

As to having children, Elsie was quite sure that she did not want any. She knew she could slip away from time to time and find some lively company; old Tom would not ask any questions. So they became, each in their own way, quite an attached couple. On Saturday evenings Elsie would go to the nearest dance hall or public house for entertainment and Tom never questioned her about her movements.

When Elsie suggested that Tom should get some help on the farm he agreed that perhaps he could do with an extra pair of hands, and yes, he had to admit that there was more than he could manage. He would think about it.

So, at the local market, Tom made some enquiries and one of his neighbours said, 'I have a cousin who is a sort of social worker. He usually knows of young men looking for work. I will ask him if he knows of a suitable lad for you.'

Chapter One

Jim Thorp sighed and said to himself, 'I should have chosen another profession, anything but the Probation Service. How often do I ever have any lasting success with my clients? But what is lasting success? Why, even doctors can't keep their patients well all the time.' These and similar thoughts passed through his mind as he drove towards Tom Draper's farm.

'Tom is a decent man. He needs a farm hand at present and if he would take on Michael Duffy, perhaps he would settle. Oh! How difficult it is to get lads into the right environment. It is not really Michael's fault that he lacks all ambition. Boys and also girls brought up in care do seem to miss out.'

As he drove through the gate and up the avenue he caught sight of Tom and waved to him. 'Hello there, Tom, how are you feeling? A bit better? I heard that you have been a little under the weather and might need some extra help. I know a fine lad who might just suit you. He tells me that he would like to work and learn farming.'

Tom, Jim knew, was a man of few words, but sound and not without a kind heart.

'Come on, then, tell me about this lad of yours.'

Jim took in the comfortable atmosphere, the bright kitchen. 'Nice place you have here,' he said.

'Aye,' replied Tom. 'The wife is out at present, but I expect she will have left my tea ready. Yes, here it is on this tray by the Aga cooker. I am sure you could do with a cup of tea after your drive from Derry. It must be all of twenty miles. Well, what can this boy do? I need help all round. If he needs to live in – which would be best because milking starts early, just after six of a morning – we could fix up two rooms over the barn beside the house. I only use the ground floor as an office and store. You would be surprised to see how much writing and paperwork there is nowadays. I think it would be better if he was separate. The rooms are quite dry; a man and his wife and child used to live up there some years ago. Some said I should have pulled those old buildings down when I put up the new milking parlour and calf houses, but I thought they might come in useful some time. Now, I think the boy would like to be a bit apart to sleep. He can come into the house for his meals. I suppose he is a Catholic, not that I mind, but I don't want any priests coming here.'

After this long speech, Tom relit his pipe and looked over to Jim, waiting for information about Michael Duffy.

Jim, as Michael's probation officer, knew that Michael was neither very good nor very bad, but that he needed a job. Fate had been against him from his earliest days when his mother had abandoned him; his father was unknown and most of his time had been spent in a children's home. He had had a period with foster parents, but this had not been satisfactory. Michael had been a shy, withdrawn boy, a low achiever at school who had grown into a passive young man without a purpose in life, rarely considering his future with any spark of ambition. A pleasant enough person who bore no resentment, there was a quality of detachment about him. Jim very sincerely hoped that he would be able to get him settled in this job with the Drapers.

'No need to worry about Michael's religion, Tom, because although he is nominally a Catholic, I don't think he practises, as they say.'

Jim was relieved that they had crossed that particular hurdle.

'Another thing – what do you mean by a training school? I thought all schools were for training.'

'Well, I am afraid Michael has been in a bit of bother and he was sent to a special school for correction and reform. Really, Tom, he did very well there. The principal personally asked me to try to get Michael into a good situation because he felt the lad should be given a chance to make something of himself. He has no family. He is a quiet boy – I am sure he will fit in well here and will give you no trouble. I can get some basic furniture for the flat.'

'No need for that. If he comes here we have enough stuff to cover all he will need; he can stay in the house until it is ready for him. When can he start?'

'I will go back and see him at the school. You can take him on a month's trial from Monday next, and also I must let you know what you will have to pay him as a trainee. With full board it won't be too much.'

Well pleased with the way the interview had gone, Jim bade Tom goodbye.

'Will see you on Monday. By the way, will Mrs Draper mind having an extra mouth to feed?'

'She will not mind. I must away to start milking – I have fifty cows to milk and young stock to feed.'

The following Monday, Jim collected Michael from the training school and drove him to Draper's farm. As they approached the farm, Jim said, 'Now, Michael, this is a good opportunity for you to make good. Be sure to do what Mr Draper asks of you. The farm is mainly a dairy farm; he tells me he has fifty milking cows and also young stock. This means that you will have to be up early every day, day in and day out. Everything has to be done correctly. Milking parlours are inspected regularly at random and if anything is amiss the farmer is fined and may lose his licence. However, it is a healthy life for those who like it. Now don't let me down – it has not been easy for me to get this position for you. Remember that you are on probation and that it is not everybody who would give you a job.'

Michael had mixed feelings about leaving the training school. He mumbled, 'Thank you, sir. I will try to give satisfaction. I think it will be better than working in a factory or on the roads. I don't have much learning – I don't know what else I could do.'

Tom and Michael suited each other well and together they fixed up the two rooms in the old barn. Michael swept away years of dust and then scrubbed the floors clean. He carried up furniture that Tom and Elsie gave him, including curtains. Michael had never before had one room to himself, let alone two; he was more than pleased with the arrangement, and said to himself, 'For the first time I have struck lucky. Old Tom is not a bad sort and Elsie, Mrs Draper, is all right. The grub is good and there is plenty of it.'

When Jim next called to see how Michael was settling in, Tom reported that the lad was a really good worker. 'I never have to tell him twice to do a thing. He is becoming useful with the milking – he seems to have a feeling for the beasts. I think he already knows each one and handles them well. I have also promised to let him drive the tractor, as I know youngsters like driving tractors. Yes, Michael is a good lad.'

Jim was very pleased and thought, I must have a word with him before I go to encourage him.

'Well, Michael, I hear Tom will make a farmer of you yet. Well done. You look very fit – the outdoor life obviously suits you. I think Tom will keep you on permanently. Learn all you can and keep out of trouble, and you will do well.'

'Thank you, sir. Would you like me to show you round the farm?'

'Yes, Michael, I would like that very much.'

'I think I had better get you a pair of rubber boots,' said Michael.

Within minutes he had produced a large pair of wellingtons. Together they inspected the large cowsheds of which Tom Draper was justifiably proud and also the modern milking parlour.

Now Michael asked, 'Would you like to see where I live? I was in the house at first but now I only go in for my meals and to use the downstairs shower and sometimes to watch TV.'

Jim was pleasantly surprised to see how tidy the two rooms were. Michael's few possessions were neatly arranged, his clothes hanging in a makeshift corner cupboard.

'It's not much, but it is mine. From this window I can see over the hills, and this one looks over the yard. Tom has lent me a donkey jacket and of course rubber boots, but I will have to get some more gear for work, as I get very wet pretty often. Mrs D dries things and does my washing – she is not a bad sort.'

'I will try to squeeze a grant for you. I can't promise but I will try. I see you get on very well with Tom, which is excellent, and I gather you also get on with Mrs Draper.'

Michael paused and then said, 'She is all right really; yes, she is okay by me. She gives me very good food, better than I have ever had before. I think she likes to cook. I love the bread she bakes and so does Tom, but she is just not the sort of person you would expect to be Tom's wife. You should see her when she is going out on Saturday nights. Her clothes are, you know, flashy, and her face is all made up and sometimes she stays away all night. Tom never seems to notice, or if he does, he never says anything to me.

Our tea is left ready, we eat, then Tom lights up his pipe and if I don't have anything more to do I might watch TV. She is always laughing at Tom and me. I just can't understand her.'

'Oh well, it is just as well she is a cheerful person and feeds you well. It is a little strange, but never mind – Tom is well pleased with you and that is the main thing.'

As he drove away, Jim mused about Tom's wife. She certainly did not sound like a likely person to be mistress of Draper's Farm. But the house was well kept as far as he could see and the boy at last seemed to be settling down pretty well. This was very satisfactory as he was almost eighteen and if he kept out of trouble he would be out of Jim's jurisdiction. Even so, he hoped Michael would do well in the future.

Left on his own, Michael smiled, as he considered Elsie, a rare character if there ever was one, with her make-up, all that hair – which changed colour frequently – and the tight clothes which accentuated her curvaceous body as she tottered about on her high heels. Still, he was not complaining, and she did him well enough. Tom and Elsie were an odd pair. No kids. Michael wondered why, and what would happen when Tom was too old to manage the farm or if he died. He must find out. He might ask Elsie. No good asking Tom. Michael never asked Tom questions, except to do with work, and Tom certainly would not answer if he did. But Elsie might talk. He would try her one Thursday when Tom was at the market.

In the meanwhile, he must get on; soon he would be needed to help Tom with milking. Two hours they would be, then perhaps he would go into the house for a cup of tea and some soda bread. Great stuff her soda bread was. All her food was good; if he did not watch it, he would be getting fat. Tom was as lean as a beanpole.

I suppose there is always so much to do from early morning until after evening, milking and then sometimes extra if a cow is calving, or whatever, thought Michael, but all in all he thought he liked it the way it was and Tom never harassed him. I must say, Elsie is a strange one.

As time went by, Michael knew he was becoming really useful to Tom. Usually, without being told, he knew exactly what he should be doing. He found that he liked working in the milking parlour; he had now no problems with the apparatus.

Michael thought how strange it was that at first all the cows had looked the same to him and that now he knew each cow in the herd; he knew their particular habits, which cow was biddable and which might show bad temper if her routine was disturbed in the slightest way.

He thought, I like to see them coming ambling in with their udders almost bursting, from the fields and later returning to their grazing sedately lowing as they move on. Strange life that of a cow, but I suppose it is all right; they have no problems. Everything is arranged for them. Even though they do miss their calves when they are first taken away from them, they seem to get over it pretty well, but I always feel sorry for them, poor beasts.

Occasionally at such times Michael's thoughts turned to his own situations. He wondered about his mother. Why had she left him? Perhaps, like the cows, she had no choice.

'I wonder what she was like, and what it would have been to have a proper mother and father and to live in a proper house. It might have been fine. I hope my mother did not look like Elsie. I don't think I would have minded having old Tom as my dad, he is all right, although he does not say much. Still, it is no good thinking about all that now. It is not too bad here, in fact I like it. Plenty to do and nobody to hassle you.'

Sometimes he wondered if he should ask Tom if he could go and play football with some lads from the nearby village.

I am sure he would let me off on a Saturday, he thought. But then he thought, I am not sure I can be bothered with football. I get all the exercise I need here and I am not sure I want to get mixed up with that crowd. I will wait a while – there is plenty of time and I don't want folk coming up here. Maybe I like things as they are. There is a lot to be said for keeping to oneself and not getting involved with anybody.

Meanwhile, Elsie, always full of energy and always looking for new sources of her particular kind of entertainment, began to see Michael in a new light. In the time that he had been working on the farm, he had filled out. The physical work had muscled him up and now he was tanned and extremely fit-looking. Elsie began to find Michael very attractive and set about seducing him. She was pretty sure that he was inexperienced with women. Soon she was contriving ways of being alone with him. Often she would bring him out a cup of tea if he was working on his own, or she would ask him to bring in some logs or a bucket of coal.

On Thursdays Tom used to go to the nearby market, even if he did not have any animals to sell; he would go to see how the market was doing. On these days he would have a hot dinner at the mart. Sometimes he took Michael with him but more often than not he left him with tasks to be undertaken. One Thursday, Elsie produced beer with dinner and she refilled his glass as he drank thirstily; it was a warm day.

'Thank you,' said Michael as he was about to leave and return to work. But Elsie blocked his way.

'What about a kiss as thanks for the beer?'

The unexpected heat and the beer had dulled Michael's ability to think clearly. As she pushed herself up against

Michael, he took her in his arms, kissing her on the mouth, while his hands found her full breasts under her blouse. He was not quite clear about exactly what followed, but when it was over, Elsie appeared to be pleased.

'We must do this again,' she said.

Michael felt physically satisfied, but suddenly he felt disgusted with himself and with Elsie. He realised that he did not even like her and thereafter he tried to avoid being alone with her. He was in a love-hate situation. On the following Thursday he did find himself alone with her, Tom being at the market as usual, and he despised himself for allowing her again to entice him into having her own way with him against his better judgement. Thereafter, Elsie's image haunted him. Clearly she was oversexed, with no morals and no loyalty to Tom who was a decent, if dull, man, but Elsie's alluring body aroused a lust in Michael which, after a few beers, he was too weak to resist.

'No, this cannot go on.'

Michael decided to move away. He was genuinely very sorry as he knew he had a good life on the farm. It had suited him for almost two years and it had been better than anything he had ever previously experienced, but he did not know how to resist Elsie's advances. Michael knew he could not face Tom if he ever found out; there was nothing he could do but get right away. He said nothing to Tom or to Elsie, but gathered together his few belongings and left, leaving no word because he just did not know what he could have said to Tom, who had always treated him so fairly.

Tom was surprised and sorry when he found Michael had gone, but knowing there were always plenty of young men seeking work he did nothing to find Michael to persuade him to come back. As for Elsie, she never mentioned Michael again.

Michael was fortunate to find employment and lodgings, and because he was a good and hard worker, who was willing to and could turn his hand to most jobs on a farm, he was usually in work, finding casual work labouring between farm work.

Chapter Two

It was several months before Elsie realised that she was pregnant and she was not pleased, as a baby was the last thing she wanted. Suspecting that Michael Duffy was the father, she thought it would be best if she passed it off as Tom's if she could get away with it. Elsie took the necessary steps to accomplish this by inviting Tom into her bed. When she told Tom that she was pregnant, she was not quite sure if he accepted that the baby was his or not, because he said very little beyond asking when the child was due and whether she was feeling all right.

Elsie reflected that Tom was never one to say much and he was not making any fuss, so she should consider herself lucky. Oh God, she really did not want the bother of a child but it was now too late to get rid of it, so she would make the best of it.

When the time came, Elsie's labour was prolonged and difficult. Elsie was exhausted and showed no interest when a midwife finally handed her the baby, saying, 'Come on, dear, you have a lovely baby boy.'

Elsie opened her eyes and thought, You are far from lovely, you look so angry.

She knew she was expected to say something, so she said, 'What does it weigh?' She wished she could have something stronger to drink than the cup of sweet tea the nurse had offered her. 'Can I go to sleep now?'

Elsie closed her eyes and drifted into a deep sleep. When she awoke she was aware of a baby crying and she wondered if it was her baby, thinking, 'How can anything so small make so much noise?'

One week later Elsie and the baby returned to the farm. Elsie felt quite unlike her usual self and was glad to be home, away from the hospital and the bossy nurses, and glad to have a smoke without their disapproving looks. She wished the child would stop crying.

Tom looked at the baby and said, 'A fine boy. What are you going to call him?'

'Robert.'

'Very good. I must away now.'

As the days passed, Elsie found she was quite unable to experience any maternal feelings for baby Robert. Every time he cried, which he did very frequently, it jarred her nerves and alarmed her. All she could think of was how she could stop the crying, the piercing screams which filled the house. Robert was a finicky feeder and would take a little of his bottle and then fall asleep, only to wake after a short time and start crying again. Although Elsie grew stronger, she felt depressed; she often found herself weeping for no reason. She felt trapped. Nothing she did seemed to lift the sensation of gloominess which enveloped her. She was listless whereas formerly she always had endless energy, weighted down now by the endless crying. Tom was unaware that anything was wrong and went about his daily chores on the farm as usual; if he noticed the sparse meals Elsie provided for him he did not say anything.

When baby Robert was six weeks old, Elsie was convinced that the baby did not like her and that he was allergic to her, and she knew she did not love him. Moreover, she felt frightened because she could not trust herself not to harm him when he screwed up his face, waved his arms wildly and arched his back screaming as if possessed with a demon. She did not know why but suddenly she knew she would never make a competent, let alone loving, mother.

Elsie gathered a few of Robert's baby clothes, feeding bottles and food, put him in his carrycot, called a taxi and asked the driver to wait for her while she went and knocked on Jean Ferguson's door. Elsie thrust the carrycot into a very surprised Jean's arms, saying, 'Please, Jean, take care of this child. I have to go away for a while. Tom will be in touch with you.'

'Come in, Elsie, you look all in.'

'I have a taxi waiting. I must be going.'

As Elsie went, she turned and saw Jean lift the infant from his basket she cradle him in her arms, making cooing noises and kissing his hands. Elsie thought, Why can't I do that? Fearing she might weep, she added, 'Thank you, Jean,' and rushed to the taxi which took her to the bus station in Londonderry. From there she went to the airport at Belfast. While waiting for her flight to London to be called, she wrote to Tom, telling him where the baby was.

Tom,

I am sorry I can't stay at the farm. I am not cut out to be a mother. Don't try and contact me, because I am never coming back. You and Robert will be better off without me. Goodbye.

Elsie

As she posted the letter, her flight was called. She boarded without allowing herself to think about Tom or the baby. Some hours later she checked in at a small hotel near Swiss Cottage.

At the reception the manageress, very much to her surprise asked, 'Would you be interested in a temporary job here? We have a vacancy in the dining room.'

Elsie could hardly believe her good fortune. Sometimes when off duty she occasionally thought about the baby and Tom, but she did not allow herself to dwell on them too much, always telling herself Jean would look after Robert and Tom would hardly miss her.

Jean Ferguson contacted Tom and promised to look after Robert until Elsie returned. She could hardly believe it when Tom said Elsie had gone for good. 'How could she abandon a baby like that?'

She went on to explain that she now had a part-time job and that they needed the extra money to keep the two boys at college so, much as she would like to have Robert permanently, she could not. After a week, when there was no word from Elsie, Jean's husband insisted that Tom would have to make alternative arrangements. He did not want Jean keeping the baby. Sorrowfully, Jean told Tom this. She had made some enquiries and heard of a Mrs Doherty who fostered babies and was said to be wonderfully good to them. Tom was at such a loss and had absolutely no idea what he should do that he gladly agreed to go and see Mrs Doherty. She agreed to take Robert, but said she only kept her babies until they were one year old because she only catered for infants and then usually in emergencies.

Robert thrived with Mrs Doherty. Tom visited every Saturday and the child stayed until he was nearly two years old. He was a very easy and loveable little boy. The kindly foster mother told Tom she could not manage a toddler and that she personally would try to find a suitable home for Robert. In the end, she kept Robert a further six months until he was placed in another foster home. Tom was not so satisfied with this arrangement and was considering trying to find somebody to look after Robert at home, but no such person was to be found, and he remained in his second foster home for another year.

Just after Robert's third birthday the tragedy occurred at the farm. Tom was killed in an accident with his tractor. A son, by his first marriage, inherited the farm and almost immediately sold it. He and his wife refused to take responsibility for Robert, informing the Children's Department that it was well known that he was not Tom's child and that they should get in touch with the boy's mother. As a sign of goodwill they would make a generous settlement to cover the cost of his keep but they would do nothing more. They moved away from County Derry and Robert was moved to a children's home.

Chapter Three

Louise walked slowly towards home, enjoying the spring sunshine. Everywhere looked especially lovely, the trees with the lightest of green leaves and buds about to burst into bloom; her mood was one of contentment, which is the gift of spring to most people. But quite suddenly she missed her footing and fell heavily. Pain shot through her hands and knees, the contents of her handbag and shopping basket spilled over the pavement and tears filled her eyes, partially blinding her. Slowly, with considerable pain, she started to pick herself up.

She felt as if she was being assisted by a strong arm. A male voice enquired, 'Are you all right, ma'am? Here is your handbag and here is your basket. You do look bad – let me help you. Where are you going?'

Louise looked up and saw a young man smiling at her. 'Thank you. I am all right now,' she said, although in fact she felt rather sick.

'Right, then, I will carry your shopping basket. Let me take your arm.'

Slowly and painfully they made their way to a large Edwardian house standing well back from the road in a carefully tended garden. On reaching the front door, Michael rang the bell and rapped the knocker; the door was immediately opened by a middle-aged man, whose face showed concern.

'Louise, what has happened?'

'I tripped and fell. This young man kindly came to my assistance and helped me home.'

'Are you hurt? Come in and let me see you.' Then turning to Michael he said, 'Thank you for your help. Do come and have some coffee or a cup of tea if you prefer.'

Louise somewhat recovered as the pain lessened. She looked over at Michael sitting awkwardly on the edge of his chair and said, 'I must thank you for your kindness and your help.' Then she remembered the casserole in the Aga. 'Would you like some lunch? I don't feel I can eat anything just now.'

Michael said, 'Please, ma'am.'

So, twenty minutes later, Michael and Edward sat down to beef stew and jacket potatoes, followed by apple pie and cream. Michael ate hungrily.

'What is your name, young man?'

'Michael, Mike or sometimes Mickey.'

'Well, Michael, again thank you, for your kindness.' He paused. 'My wife and I are very grateful to you. Would you be interested in a week's work? I have some jobs outside in the garden and also some painting. I could do with some help just now.'

'Thank you, sir,' said Michael. 'I am usually a farm hand but I can turn my hand to most things. I am between jobs just now. I am expecting to start a regular job in a week or so.'

'Right then, we will see you on Monday at 9 a.m.'

A few minutes later, Michael was once again out in the sunshine and on his way. He was pleased with his luck. While assisting Louise to get to her feet and to retrieve her handbag, he had slipped two five pound notes into his back pocket. He did not feel too bad about this. He reasoned she had plenty of money and he had so little. She probably would not even miss it.

Michael did not usually resent the fact that he was a poor person, which is how he now saw himself. However, if the opportunity presented itself, he took full advantage of it. He had been guilty of shoplifting and occasionally breaking into houses when he was younger.

'If people were foolish enough to leave doors and windows open and unlocked, was it not giving an open invitation to a person who was short of money?'

As a person Michael lived very much from day to day, especially since he had left Draper's Farm. He rarely looked back to his childhood and he never seriously considered his future.

On Monday, when Michael arrived at the Robinsons' house, Edward was waiting for him. After a friendly 'good morning' he showed Michael the fence that needed repairing.

'You will find a pile of timber near the garden shed, and nails and all the other things are in the shed. Should you finish that before I get back would you dig over that end flower bed?'

'Surely,' said Michael.

Edward went off and Michael set to work. At about ten thirty Louise appeared with a mug of tea and some buttered scones. 'Good morning, Michael. As you can see, I am none the worse for my fall on Saturday.'

At lunchtime Michael was called into the kitchen for a bowl of soup, home-made bread and fruit – oranges, apples and grapes, which Michael had never had before. Edward joined them, and before he returned to his office he went out with Michael to inspect his morning's work. At about three thirty, a tray of tea arrived for Michael. At five Edward returned and Michael, who was a careful worker, was about to clean and put away his tools and knock off for the day; he had enjoyed his day's work and the refreshments. This pattern continued until Friday.

Michael's efforts made an impression on the Robinsons' garden. He also painted the utility room. Louise always gave him tea mid-morning and at about three in the afternoon, as well as some soup at lunchtime, when they were joined by Edward.

The house and Edward and Louise, especially Louise, fascinated Michael. He tried to imagine the kind of life the Robinsons led and he could not. His impression was of overall calmness harmony and serenity. An air of contentment prevailed. Never before had he experienced such an atmosphere. Rarely did they engage in conversation, nor did they question him about his background or what his plans were for the future.

During one of these breaks, Louise put an extra cup on the tray, saying, 'Can I join you and enjoy the sunshine for five minutes?' She then sat down on a garden chair while Michael sat on the grass.

'Have you any family? Where do you live?'

Michael told her that he had been brought up in a children's home, that he had also spent some time with two different sets of foster parents, but that he had not stayed very long with either of them, although he remembered he had quite liked being with families. He also told her that he had been to a government training scheme before he had worked on a farm; in fact he had worked on several farms. Farm work was what he really liked best. At present he was between jobs, but he was hoping to take up a new job quite soon.

As he talked he studied Louise. Maybe about fifty years, he thought. Still quite good-looking. Her clothes seem to be just right for her, unlike Elsie's clothes, he recalled, which always looked as if they were not big enough for her and were so startling.

Louise reminded Michael a little of a lady magistrate he had once appeared before, but with much kinder eyes and an altogether softer person. That other lady, he recalled, was tough; of that he was sure. He summed Louise to be a real lady.

In exchange for this information, Louise volunteered that Edward and she had two daughters and four grandchildren. One daughter, Anne, was unmarried and worked in a large department store in London in a high-powered position. Mary, their elder daughter, was married to a farmer and they lived in County Wicklow.

After a pause, Louise said, 'We did have a son, James. He was killed in a motor accident when he was only seven. He was such a dear little boy. I don't know why I am telling you about James, because it was a very long time ago now, not that we can ever forget him. Forgive me, we love our family so much. We tend to spoil the grandchildren and indeed Mary and Anne as well; it is the privilege of growing old, you see.'

Nobody ever loved me and certainly nobody ever spoiled me, thought Michael. On reflection he realised that he had never loved anybody either. He also thought these daughters and grandchildren were fortunate to be related to Edward and Louise, especially Louise.

He decided that they lived in quite different worlds; comfortable worlds where houses were spacious, even quite grand, unlike anything he had ever come across or indeed was ever likely to be in again. Lucky for some people. He was not inclined to be envious. Really, in some unexplainable way he was glad that he had met the Robinsons because they were nice and a good sort of people. Pity about the little kid that had been killed; she still remembered him. He even was a little sorry that he had stolen some of Louise's money.

On Friday evening, Edward paid Michael £60 in cash and thanked him for a very good week's work. 'Well done,

Michael. If you are free in a few weeks' time I could most likely give you another week's work.'

Louise thanked Michael for coming to her assistance, saying that he was her 'knight in shining armour'.

Michael had been right when he recognised that the Robinsons lived in a rare atmosphere of harmony. Such was the state of their relationship, even after forty years together. Mysteriously, their love for one another was blossoming and continued to blossom, although it was now different, but no less strong, than the first love Edward had had for Louise when, as a convalescent young officer home from the Normandy landings in 1944, he had fallen head over heels in love with the pretty physiotherapist who was treating his damaged knee. The joint had been extremely slow to respond to treatment and continued to give him pain and a degree of lameness. When he was finally discharged from the Army with a small disability pension, he had married Louise and together they had returned to Londonderry and set up home. Edward had gone into his father's importing business.

Two daughters, Mary and Anne, were born, followed by a son, James. The Robinsons were not wealthy by any means, but they were comfortably off and as near to happiness as anybody can expect to be, until tragedy struck. James, aged seven years old, was killed when a car skidded on a patch of unseen ice and mounted the pavement. James was instantly killed. Louise and Edward were devastated and found it almost impossible to believe what had happened or to pick up the threads of their lives. Both became quieter, withdrawn and disinclined to take part in any form of social life, but for Mary and Anne's sakes they both made a tremendous effort not to become morose.

Behind Louise's gentle exterior was a great strength of character which allowed her to live with the pain of James's death, and as time passed this pain became less constant and gradually faded, but never completely disappeared. Eventually, she was able to look at the photographs of the smiling little boy. She bore no bitterness and she could remember how dear he had been to her and to all of them. Edward, on the other hand, had found James's death more difficult to accept and he was sustained by Louise through the terrible time following the accident. That was fifteen years ago and James now was a happy little ghost, seldom spoken of, but whose presence remained in the house causing occasional stabbing pain and, alternately, joyous memories of a little boy who had spent a few years with them and then left them. Louise, in overcoming her grief, had bestowed ever-increasing love on her family, especially on Edward, so that she and Edward were in step, one with the other, and had attained the serenity that Michael sensed but could not have put into words during the time he had worked for them. It was something that he was to remember for a very long time.

After Michael had taken his leave of the Robinsons, Louise said to Edward, 'I felt sorry for that young man. He told me he had no family and he had been brought up in children's homes and with foster parents whom he liked but had not stayed with. It is sad to think of a child growing up without anybody to love him.'

'Of course it might not be true. He could have been just spinning you a yarn. Anyhow, children's homes are perfectly all right, maybe a darn sight better than some homes. They cost the ratepayers enough.'

Chapter Four

Michael never returned to the Robinsons for work or anything else because one year later he was in Crumlin Road gaol, awaiting trial on a serious terrorist charge.

The evening after Michael had finished working for the Robinsons, he was sitting in the public bar of the Black Thorn public house, a few miles outside Londonderry. He noticed a man, who looked vaguely familiar, on the other side of the bar. The man appeared to be waiting for somebody; he kept looking towards the door. Michael was feeling relaxed as he finished his pint. He had money in his pocket and the prospect of a new job.

After a short time, this man came over and sat down beside Michael and said, 'You are Michael Duffy. Remember me? Do you remember Saturday mornings in the markets?'

Then it came back to Michael. This was Packy, a former schoolmate with whom he had played truant and, with another boy, had stolen fruit from the market stalls.

'Want to earn some of the ready?'

Michael ignored a warning feeling not to have anything to do with this man, so he accepted another drink and then another one, saying, 'What do I have to do?'

'Well, it is simple really. I was waiting for another chap but he has not showed up, so I can offer you a good thing. There is a load of building material to be collected from a quarry, not far from here. It is all fixed. I was to take Bill up there and he was to have delivered to this address.'

He produced a piece of paper.

'Bill, the bugger, has let me down. Five pound now and another when the job is done. What do you say?'

Normally Michael would not have allowed himself to be sucked into anything shady or even remotely connected with any paramilitary organisation; neither nationalist, nor loyalist. It always had seemed to him that whoever ruled the country, he would still be a poor man at the end of the day. Whatever they promised they would probably not keep their promises as likely as not, and even if they did he would not be affected. Usually he did not feel like sticking his neck out for one or the other. Orange or Green, they meant little or nothing to him. However, by this time he was rather drunk and was not seeing things too clearly. He allowed himself to be persuaded to take on this job.

Together they left the pub. As Michael got into the car he felt something hard press into his back. Now he knew that Packy was up to no good. As if to confirm this, Packy whispered, 'Just so that you understand that this job is confidential, like. You get my meaning, Michael, and there is no going back now. Well, let us go now.'

They drove off into the darkness.

After about twenty minutes they arrived at the quarry. There was, at first sight, no sign of anybody; no lights in the Portakabin which was the works office. Packy sounded his horn three times and a small van appeared and drew up alongside.

'That you, Jim?' said Packy. 'This here is Michael, who is willing to take the goods yonder. Got the papers? Okay, give them to Michael. Away with you, just take the van to this address. Any enquiries, you are delivering a special order of gravel to be used in a landscaping job which McGurk's Building Merchants have on order.'

He gave Michael a folded document. As an afterthought he added, 'Have you a driving licence? Well, if asked just say it is in the pocket of another anorak and you can get it if necessary.'

Michael, quite sober by now, realised that this was no ordinary load of gravel and hoped that he would not be stopped by the RUC or by the Army. As he got out of Packy's car once again, he felt the muzzle of a gun being poked into the small of his back. 'Mind now, Mike, all that I have told you.'

With a feeling of impending doom, Michael drove away from the quarry. He had almost reached the builders' yard when he was flagged down by a roving Army patrol. What followed happened very quickly. The papers he produced did not satisfy the corporal, who asked Michael to step out of the van and open up the back. A couple of soldiers climbed in; one had a sniffer dog and they uncovered numerous bags of gravel when the dog stopped at one and became very excited, whining and pawing it. The soldiers immediately recognised that this bag was different from all the others and contained what they knew to be explosive material and not what was listed on Michael's papers. In vain, he tried to protest and say explosives were on order and were legitimate, but the corporal would not accept this. Michael watched as they went through the entire load. He knew it would be useless to try to run away. He was horrified and very frightened.

'You are under arrest.' With that he was bundled into the Army jeep and taken to the nearest police station where he spent a sleepless night in the cells. He never knew what became of the van or its load, and he never heard again from Packy Coyle.

Next morning he was brought before the magistrates, he was charged with being in possession of explosive material and ordered to be kept in custody to await trial. Later that day he was transferred to the remand wing at Crumlin Road Prison in Belfast, under guard.

Shortly after arrival at the prison his position was explained to him. He could see a solicitor and have brief daily visits while on remand. He could wear his own clothes and have food sent in. He would not be required to work, except to keep his cell clean and tidy.

Michael, who had always considered himself to be fairly tough, was gripped by despair. He knew he was trapped and he blamed himself. Of course he should have known that Packy was up to no good. He recalled how years ago he had urged him to go to the market and had shown him how to steal fruit from the stalls. He should never have allowed himself to be taken advantage of when he was dulled by drink. Self-pity at first took possession of him, but later he realised the gravity of his situation. He knew he was guilty of a serious terrorist crime. He felt bitter because he had no feelings of loyalty to any cause. At heart he was no terrorist. His despair became more and more enveloping.

A visit from the prison chaplain did nothing to relieve these feelings or lift his spirits, as the priest reminded Michael bluntly that he should be grateful that he person-ally was not responsible for the deaths of innocent people – women and children and pensioners – and the destruction of homes and businesses, to say nothing of putting unfortunate people on the dole.

'Think about that, young man. No use now saying that you had taken drink. This does not absolve you of your responsibilities.'

The chaplain had touched on a raw and sensitive nerve in Michael's make-up. He was haunted by the priest's words. Nothing in his surroundings helped in any way. He felt absolutely suicidal. There was no future for him. The present was becoming almost unbearable. The noise on the wing where he was held seemed shattering to his frayed nerves; the officers appeared remote and unfeeling, issuing orders, locking and unlocking doors. Michael was amazed that so many of his fellow prisoners on remand seemed to be adjusted to the routine and were optimistic about the result of their court appearances; some were not too concerned about the outcome but were more concerned as to where they would eventually serve their time. Michael could not relate to them. He felt for him life was just not worth living. He wished he could die and end it all. But he did not know how to set about taking his life and in any case he would not have the nerve to accomplish such a thing.

Chapter Five

Michael never knew how he existed during the months he was on remand, alternately totally miserable or merely bored. He longed for the fresh air of his former life; he found the exercise yard to be a bleak and rather dirty area surrounded by high walls with barred windows of the other wings. Nothing green and not much fresh air. He felt suffocated, always with an intense longing to get out and away into the country. Having no family, he had no visitors except his solicitor and the chaplain. After his first visit, the chaplain was never again so accusing or harsh with Michael. He did try, not very successfully, to comfort him.

'Would you like to make your confession?'

Michael, never religious, thanked him but declined. He did not say, 'I do not feel it would be any use either to me or you.'

Father McRory did not press the matter. Leaving, he said, 'Bless you, my son. I am always here if you need me.'

One day, a kindly, middle-aged man visited him. He found Michael just sitting looking into space. As he closed the door he said, 'Michael, I hear you have no visitors. I am a member of the St Vincent de Paul Society. We try to help people with all kinds of problems. Most often we help the poor and needy with material things like cash or food, clothing and bits and pieces of furniture. We also like to befriend the lonely and people in prison. No strings attached. My name is Joe and I would like to be your friend.'

Michael was feeling particularly depressed and had to make quite an effort to say in a small, dull voice, 'Thank you. You are very kind.'

Joe continued, 'Tell me a little about yourself. What did you do before you came here?'

'Well, I worked on a farm. I liked to be out in the open and I miss being out there. The other men don't seem to mind being closed in but I can't cope being shut in all the time. I know that it is all my own fault and I should not complain but sometimes I feel that I will go mad, and at other times I wish I were dead. That would be better than this hateful cell.'

He sighed deeply again, saying, 'I know I should not grumble because it is my own fault,' and slowly he told Joe how he had met up with Packy, got rather drunk and then allowed himself to be persuaded to do a job which, had he been in his right mind, he would never have touched. He was caught with explosives hidden in a load of gravel. Well, here he was and he did not care one jot for the IRA or any other organisation.

Joe looked long and hard at Michael. That was the way the IRA got young and foolish men to do their dirty work for them and, as in Michael's case, get caught while they remained at large to set up another so-called 'exercise on active service'. No words of comfort came to Joe.

'Do you know, Michael, I have been walking around this prison for the last two hours and my feet ache? Can I sit and rest a while with you and have a smoke? Do you smoke? No? Well, have some chocolate. Come on, I expect it is some time since you had any chocolate, or do you buy some? You can, you know, in the tuck shop or as a remand prisoner you can send out for food. No alcohol, of course, which is what you would like from time to time, I suppose,' he added with a grin.

Michael was quite taken aback by Joe's approach. He accepted this little man as a friend, who was on his side. He seemed so ordinary and so human. He felt he could relate to him. He accepted some chocolate and it tasted very good. The ice was broken and they chatted easily until it was time for Joe to go. Before he knocked on the door, which was the signal for the officer to open up and let him out, Joe promised to come on the following weekend and bring some paper books.

He added very casually, 'By the way, are you a Catholic? Not that it matters.'

Michael, somewhat uneasy for the first time during Joe's visit, replied, 'I should be, but somehow I don't feel anything. I was never any good at praying.'

'We could say a short prayer together, you and me, but if you don't feel like it, never mind. I will get my wife to say one for both of us. She is a great one for praying. Nobody has faith like my Mary, so that takes care of that.'

Just as he was about to leave, he shook hands with Michael and was gone. When he was alone again Michael's eyes pricked with tears. He was so touched that Joe had shaken hands with him, as though he was an ordinary person and not a criminal. Joe, he felt, was indeed a friend. He did not know exactly why, but he felt uplifted, his spirit less bruised by Joe's visit, affected in a way that neither the chaplain, his solicitor nor the Board of Visitors had done. He was still weighted down by his guilt.

Michael ate little and slept badly. He asked if he could do some work. The wing officer, remarking that it was unusual for remand prisoners to request to work, said he would arrange for him to join a work party. He was allotted some preparing of walls for redecorating and he felt this saved his sanity.

Joe came every weekend. He brought papers with farming news. He encouraged Michael to talk and for the most part he just listened, puffing away on his pipe. Over and over again Michael would say he blamed himself for his situation.

He knew he was guilty, but he felt bitter because he had never cared about politics. He would always be a poor man and now he was not even a free man. Joe never preached to Michael; he heard him out because he felt Michael needed to unburden himself.

When Michael came to a full stop, Joe would say, 'Now, Michael, let us look forward. What can be done to help? You won't be here always. At present you have a great deal of time on your hands, even though you go out with a work party. Painting isn't it? Which you tell me you find useful for filling in the time and keeping boredom at bay, but I would like to help you to do something which will be of use to you later on. Oh yes, that time will come. I know it seems a long way off now, but it will come and you must be prepared for it: look forwards and not backwards.'

Michael listened incredulously, and Joe continued, 'Now, in here you have time and you could develop a strong reading habit. I will bring you books and we can discuss them when I come each week. I know you say that you never read much, but now is the time to start. I can lay my hands on all kinds of books – adventure, nature, romance, westerns, war stories and so on. There is no end to the choice that there is open to you. What do you say?'

'Well, I just don't know. I was a duffer at school, but if you think I could take to reading, I will give it a try.'

'Let me tell you a little about myself. I was no good at school either. My sister was the clever one in our family; she went on to be a teacher. I thought I would go into my father's business, just like that. It was a fruit and vegetable shop and quite successful, but my father was a wise man and he said unless I went to night school and learnt book-keeping and business management he would not have me

in the shop. At first I found this difficult and boring. I
wished that I had been more attentive at school and less
idle. However, I stuck it out, with encouragement from my
mother. Now, of course, I am glad because I own the shop
and there is more to this than just handing over fruit and
veg. So, you see, you must take up something while you are
here.'

Joe brought a selection of books and left them with
Michael. Thereafter, each week they discussed them.

'Did you like the one about the horse? *Black Beauty*. It is
a children's classic but my sister thought you would like it.'

'I was near to shedding a tear or two, it was so sad.
Imagine folk being so cruel to dumb beasts.'

'How indeed, people can be very cruel. Sometimes they
just don't think. And did you like *Robinson Crusoe*? I will
bring you some more adult books now that you have got
into the way of reading. I think we will try Dickens next.
These are very long but excellent reading. Also remember,
Michael, there is a prison library if ever I can't get in to see
you.'

Michael said, 'I never thought I would read and enjoy
them so much. It has made such a difference to me.'

'Now, there is something else, Michael. After your trial
you will almost certainly be transferred to another prison
and there will be opportunities for you to take educational
classes and even get some qualifications. Reading will not
be enough, but the habit will stand you in good stead.
Promise me, Michael, you will do this.'

Joe's visits were the highlights of Michael's week. The
modest little man with his quiet manner each week left
Michael feeling in better spirits, less bitter and altogether
calmer. Joe had somehow restored his self-confidence and
he felt better equipped to face his coming trial and was less
afraid of the future, when, after almost twelve months, two

things had happened that set Michael back considerably. A different St Vincent de Paul volunteer came in Joe's place.

'Michael I am afraid that I have some bad news for you. Joe died during the week. Joe often spoke to us about you. He told us how well you had overcome your deep depression and also how you were developing good reading habits. He had grown very close to you.'

Michael could hardly believe what he was hearing. He felt a terrible sense of loss not to see Joe every weekend. He did not know how he would get through the weeks and months ahead.

His visitor said, 'Somebody from the St Vincent de Paul will be keeping in touch with you. I know Joe will be hard to follow, but we will not desert you. It is well known that Joe was a very special person. All I can say to you is that you were privileged to have known him, which is how we all feel.' But Michael was not really listening. The lasting effect of Joe's death on Michael had been to imbue him with a certain moral strength; he had inspired him with a hope and a degree of confidence.

The man who replaced Joe was kindly, but he never got through to Michael and was little comfort to him.

The second thing which occurred about this time was that Michael's solicitor was able to give him the date for his trial – just three weeks ahead. He promised to advise and brief him how to plead, going to some pains to explain the court proceedings. He said that Michael would have a lawyer to represent him in court, and that nearer the time he would have an interview with this lawyer. He thought Michael would be advised to plead guilty.

Michael was still grieving for Joe and he was unable to pay too much attention. He had been in custody for almost thirteen months, the longest and worst he could remember. He had lost his friend and had become dispirited again.

Sometimes at night he could see Joe's stocky figure and hear his soft voice saying 'Michael, hold on, don't give in. Look forward not back,' this was one of his favourite sayings, and Michael would try to fight his depression. At other times he thought he heard Joe saying, 'Even in prison, humanity exists.'

After thirteen months his trial eventually came up. He knew what the outcome would be. There would be little in his defence that could take away from the seriousness of the charge against him. In spite of the damaging circumstances, the system required that Michael should stand trial before a judge, but at this time not a jury. His solicitor explained to him that every aspect of his case would be most carefully considered and thoroughly aired.

On the day, Michael stood in the dock between two prison officers, feeling quite alone, miserable, nervous and unnerved by the proceedings. An elderly, stern-looking judge and gowned and wigged men, whom he was given to understand were lawyers, would argue his case. Others he did not know kept bobbing up and down and whispering to each other.

His solicitor was there too. He had advised Michael to plead guilty when the time came. Michael saw the judge looking over his spectacles and making notes. Strangely, he could see quite clearly that the judge used an old fountain pen and that he had several similar pens lined up in front of him, as though he did not trust the modern biro type of pen for his note-taking.

Michael felt more and more nervous. He was not questioned beyond being asked how he pleaded. For this he felt relieved.

At length it was time for the summing up. Michael's counsel, standing up, hands tucked into the front of his gown and facing the judge, commenced by pleading lack of responsibility on Michael's part because 'he had been pressurised by a person or persons unknown when he was a little drunk. These persons had plied him with strong drink, which he was unaccustomed to, and they had taken advantage of him. They had pressed him into a driving job, as a favour, saying that they had been let down by their regular driver. They had not, truthfully, told him what the load contained.'

He went on to say that 'Michael was quite unaware of the nature of the mission he had undertaken.' Also that 'he was not and never had been a member of any illegal organisation. He was an orphan. Furthermore, he was a disadvantaged person, never having had the support and love of a family. He had already been in prison for over a year, which was a great hardship for him because he was an agricultural worker, used to being out in the open and not confined.' Michael's counsel trusted his Lordship would take all these points into consideration.

Michael listened and hoped, but doubted that the judge would be influenced by such eloquence. These doubts were confirmed when the counsel for the Prosecution demolished any and all mitigating circumstances and presented Michael as 'a hard and greedy, wicked terrorist who deliberately went out to kill and maim any number of innocent people, and would have done so if, most fortunately, he had not been caught red-handed and rightly held in custody'.

After this, Michael knew his case was lost and he tried to brace himself for whatever sentence the judge would give him.

'Michael Duffy, I find you guilty of a very serious charge, that of handling explosives. I will accept that you were not altogether sober at the time, but that does not absolve you from the result of your actions. I accept that you are not formally a member of an illegal organisation; nevertheless, you were caught in possession of a load of explosives, which could have done untold damage to life and property, and therefore I sentence you to ten years in prison.'

Chapter Six

Michael was returned to Crumlin Road Prison across the road from the courts by an underground passageway. This time he was a committed prisoner and housed in a different wing. The following day he had a medical examination and was assessed as to his educational ability and his suitability for work. He described himself as an agricultural worker and requested to be given outdoor work. No promises were made but it was noted in his file. Within two weeks he was transferred to Magilligan Prison.

Here he immediately found conditions more acceptable than the claustrophobic atmosphere of the Victorian Crumlin Road. He found that the modern prison, formerly an Army camp, had three new permanent blocks in the form of an 'H' recently added; completed, each block housed one hundred men. The blocks were subdivided into four wings, in which the men had their living quarters, one man to a cell. At first the place seemed enormous but Michael soon got to know the layout. There were work-shops and playing fields and he was told there was a hospital and a punishment block. Michael shivered and hoped he would never see the inside of either. In spite of the fact that every building was enclosed in a vast wire cage, the entrances manned by an officer at all times, Michael did not find it too oppressive. There was ample fresh air.

Twice every day the men left their blocks and went to work. They were provided with donkey jackets for bad weather; Magilligan was very exposed and the wind almost continually howled and whistled through the wire cages, except when it was fine weather when it was very hot as the sun was reflected off the concrete. The men complained about the weather, whether it was wet and cold or very hot. Michael did not mind; in fact he found all the fresh air reminiscent of his former life and so much more acceptable to him than Crumlin Road.

At first Michael worked in the wood yard, chopping logs. The work was hard, but he did not object. He was tired at the end of each session. He found he was eating and sleeping better; he even found that he was looking forward to his meals. Unlike his fellow inmates, he did not find fault with the food. Because he had no expectations he was neither disappointed nor discontented. He tried to avoid confrontations with other prisoners. He watched TV and played the occasional game of pool. He took books from the library when the librarian visited his wing, but he was at a loss to choose without any guidance and he did not always choose well. He received no mail and had no visits. He was always quiet and caused the staff no problem. He gradually became accustomed to the regime. He was made wing orderly, which suited him very well. He kept himself to himself; it was recognised that he was a loner. He made no special friends and thought that he had no enemies, but this was not the case.

At this time there was general discontent. Prisoners on both sides of the political divide felt very strongly that they should be housed in separate quarters, the more so because in other Northern Ireland prisons loyalists and republicans, or nationalists, were kept apart and they knew it. However, at Magilligan the authorities were equally adamant that all inmates should be integrated on the wings, at work and at association. In fact, they would not permit the all-weather football pitches to be used unless there were more or less equal numbers of Catholics and Protestants, that was nationalists and loyalists. Ringleaders continually strove to deepen the divide, and if they felt inmates were weakening on the issue, every kind of ploy, including collusion, was called into play to keep the protest and ensuing discontent going. Anyone like Michael, unwilling to comply, was given a hard time.

On two occasions he was beaten up, once fairly severely, because he had categorically refused to be drawn into a protest of long standing, organised by paramilitary inmates demanding the segregation which the authorities were refusing to grant. As an orderly, the ringleaders knew Michael could get his hands on information which could be of use to them, but Michael wanted no part of their ruse. Before giving up on him as a non-starter, they decided to make him sorry he had not gone along with their disruptive plans.

One evening in the washrooms, two men came up from behind, hit him on the head and then held his head in the basin of water until he was unable to struggle or call out. They might have held him under the water until he expired, except that just before this happened another prisoner came in whereupon they let Michael go and disappeared, but not before Michael's rescuer had seen who his tormentors were. This man immediately called an officer and together they half carried Michael to the chief's office and called up the hospital for help.

Michael, though very shaken, soon recovered. He was excused all duties for the rest of that day. Next day Michael and his rescuer were very closely questioned about the incident; neither men said they had seen anything but the assailants' backs and that all had taken place so quickly that they had no idea of either of their identities and so, without witnesses, the matter went no further. After that, Michael was left to his own devices. He polished the floors until they were almost dangerous underfoot; he kept the outside yards very clean and tidy. As an orderly he earned a degree of respect from the officers on his wing.

About this time he was approached by the education officer and offered various options which he could study in his spare time and even full time. He was about to say he did not think he could cope with any form of education, that he had been hopeless at school, but suddenly Joe's advice, so often repeated, came back to him.

He fancied that he heard Joe saying, 'Come on, Michael, here is a door opening for you. Go ahead – take up art classes. You could draw quite well. You used to like art at school, remember?' The voice faded away but Michael knew what he must do.

'Well, what about it?'

Michael answered, 'I think I would like to try the art classes. Art was about the only thing I was any good at when I was at school.'

Michael added his name to those already on the board. He noted that the classes would be held every Tuesday. If the class officer was notified that an inmate was allotted a place, he could be excused from normal work for that time. Two weeks later Michael received a form which informed him that he had been accepted for art classes, starting on the following Tuesday.

When he arrived at the education block he was directed to a Portakabin which was fitted out as an art classroom. Seven other men were already at work, laboriously painting with watercolours. They hardly looked up as Michael came in. The art mistress, a bespectacled, middle-aged lady, came over to him and took his form.

'Welcome to our group.'

Nobody had ever said 'welcome' to Michael. Was he dreaming? Surely this art teacher would soon be barking orders at him as the other officers did, but no. She continued, 'I see, Michael Duffy, you wish to take up Art. What have you done before?'

'I have not done very much since I left school, but I thought I would like to try my hand at drawing and painting. I was not too bad at school.'

'Right then, sit over here. Here is the drawing paper and pencils. Perhaps you can start by sketching this jug with the branch and dried daisies.'

Michael sat down, looking at his classmates, all very quiet and seemingly intent on their own work.

Michael thought, A brown earthenware jug with a dead branch and dead flowers; what a daft thing to draw, but then he must not annoy this lady teacher who seemed to be so nice. If this is what she wants, this is what I shall try to do.

He settled down to work and before long he had produced a reasonable sketch. The shelf and its contents, he felt, were not too bad, but somehow he could not get the jug or the shelf as he would have liked. When he finished, he put down his pencil and waited for Mrs Moore to come and see it.

Mary Moore was a dedicated teacher. She had come to teaching fairly recently, to augment her income when her son had become a medical student at Edinburgh and made many demands on her clergyman husband's salary. She was an artist of no mean standing. She could have made more money if she had sold more of her work. She loved painting, mainly in watercolours, and was always reluctant to sell her pictures, though she frequently gave them away. At first she had been concerned as to whether she would be able to handle a class of prisoners, and she was quite surprised to find how amenable these grown men were when she first took charge of the class. Prison Officer Ferguson was amazed at the ease with which she controlled the class.

Ferguson often thought, This wee woman could teach the other officers and instructors a thing or two. Fancy saying to the lads, 'I hope you enjoy our classes. We use first names here. I look forward to getting to know you all.'

They had all settled to work as meekly as lambs; not a single wisecrack and never a sound all through the session. These burly youngsters, for none were more than in their early twenties, responded by being respectful and obviously pleased that they had come, even if none showed any great talent. Drawing and especially working with colours seemed to have a calming effect on them. They listened to what Mary had to say and asked her advice as to how to improve. A few took up calligraphy and became very good at it, which was satisfying to them and to Mary, as their teacher. When Michael joined the group, they were about to start making Christmas cards.

When Mary finally came to inspect Michael's drawing, she studied it carefully bending down. 'A very good start. I see you draw quite well. I think you will enjoy these classes.'

In the weeks that followed, Michael found himself looking forward to Tuesday's classes. Mary soon recognised that Michael had talent. She encouraged him and praised his every effort. She introduced him to calligraphy, because she thought he could practise in his cell during the long periods of lock-up. Michael mastered this very quickly. Mary took great pains with all her pupils, even those who showed little promise, but she found Michael was different. He could draw freehand easily and accurately, but his work showed little imagination.

When she suggested he should do some drawing in his cell, he would say, 'But there is nothing there to draw.'

'Nonsense,' she replied. 'Close your eyes and try to recall all the things you were familiar with before you came here. What did you do out there?'

'Well, I was a farmhand.'

'Well then, you would be able to picture things around the farm: animals, buildings, machinery, the farmhouse. There is material to keep you going for as long as you are here. Or if that does not appeal to you, look at the furniture in your cell. Subjects like chairs and tables and such mundane objects provide very good exercise and practice. Now I will get you, and anybody else who is interested, drawing paper and pencils and perhaps paints and you all can do homework after lock-up and then bring it back next time and we can discuss it together.'

At first Michael was too shy to produce any of his work, but when the others brought their efforts, he did eventually bring some of his drawings and sketches for Mary to see. She was not disappointed, and even more pleased when suddenly, one week, he brought some startling pictures and some abstracts.

'You see,' he said, 'I think I am getting the hang of it. I now have paints in my cell. I like using colours. I can't explain very well, but it helps me to think of a subject and then get it down on the paper. The different colours show, at least to me, how I am feeling.'

Mary felt a glow of satisfaction. How very rarely did she have a pupil who showed such promise. To think Michael was a prisoner. What a pity! She wondered if he would ever fulfil his potential.

'Michael,' she said, 'if you are to develop your drawing there is a great deal you must learn. You must study certain aspects and disciplines. These will be quite difficult but I will help you all I can and advise you as you go along. You must learn about human anatomy, perspective, the effects of light and shade on space, and much more. It is not enough to be able to draw well. I can suggest books for you to get from the library. You will manage if you take it step by step. You have ability and also time for study and practice.'

'I never thought there could be so much to drawing,' said Michael.

'You never thought. I am afraid most of you never thought carefully enough.' But Mary was very pleased with the way Michael was shaping.

She knew he spent a great deal of time at this work when he was alone, also that he read the books she recommended. She was pleased to note that he was unaffected by the comments made by some of his fellow classmates when they saw the art books.

Eventually, Mary Moore approached the education officer about Michael. 'I have a really talented young man in my art class. Can we utilise his talent in any way? You see, he tells me he has no family, that he gets no visits or any mail. So, you see, there is no outlet for his work.'

'Well, Mary, I don't see what I can do for him. He is your baby.'

'Come on now, George. We cannot let him just fade away. Can't you commission pictures for the staff, the offices or perhaps the visiting areas here or in some of the other establishments, or a mural.'

'Now, Mary, you know what a very tight budget I have to work with.'

Some days later, George met Mary as she was walking to her class. 'I have been thinking about your budding artist. Perhaps he could do some posters for the visiting centre which has just been refurbished, at great expense I might add. Posters for the main visiting hall and for the kiddies' corner, which is a new addition. Also the waiting rooms are very dismal. I might be able to get a small amount of cash for this – mind you, it would be a very small amount, just enough to cover paper and paint. If his work is as good as you say it is, his pictures could be framed in the carpentry work shop.'

On the following Tuesday Mary told Michael about her plans for him. He was a little alarmed at the idea of going public, as it were, but he was also pleased.

Mary added, 'I have been thinking. Perhaps you should try for your City and Guilds. It would be useful to you later on.'

Mary discussed ideas for posters, starting with the children's posters, and finally came up with the theme taken from a farmyard with the emphasis on young animals. At the same time, Michael was excused from his duties as orderly for several hours each weekday.

Chapter Seven

After a time Michael earned a small degree of respect from the prison staff because he worked hard and caused them no problems. He did not disrupt the daily routine and he had never been on a charge for any misdemeanour. On the recommendation of the chief officer on his wing, his request to work out of doors was granted. He joined the gardens work party, which usually consisted of trusted inmates who worked in the grounds surrounding the 'H' blocks. The authorities were trying to improve the general appearance by landscaping the campus. Any area which lent itself to this was planted out with grass and raised flower beds. There were also several glasshouses where seeds were raised, later to be transplanted. They also grew tomatoes and lettuces which the staff could buy, but did not raise enough for the prisoners' kitchens. Michael found this work much to his liking. He got on well with the other men in the garden party. It was quite an acceptable option. He even fussed when he could not get away from the block to water his seedlings because for one reason or another there was no officer to oversee the gardeners.

Michael continued with his weekly art classes, but the project of the posters for the visiting complex did not materialise, much to Mary Moore's dismay and to a lesser extent to Michael's.

This was a period when tensions were very high in all the prisons in Northern Ireland. In one establishment prisoners were refusing to conform to prison rules; they were demanding political status. To that end, large numbers were refusing to wash or to use the normal toilet facilities, fouling their cells and wearing only a blanket.

Ten men went on hunger strike and carried their protest to the ultimate end, which was a very long and very distressing affair for everyone remotely concerned with prisons, for their families, all prison staff, prisoners and the public. The world's media followed the unfolding tragedy of wasted young lives. No one, not even Michael Duffy who had no political affiliations, could but be affected. At the death of the first hunger striker, many prisoners remained in their cells as a mark of respect, as they saw it. Magilligan was tense but calm. The staff kept a low profile and handled the matter with great sensitivity. Michael found working in the gardens very calming and he was able to keep himself very much to himself, which was the way he wanted it to be.

One day while in the greenhouse, one of his fellow gardeners asked him what he had done before he came inside. Michael related, for the first time, that he had been a farm hand and that he hoped, on his release, he would somehow be able to work again on the land. Michael became quite friendly with this man who was housed in another wing from him. Because they both worked well, the officer overlooking the garden party gave them their instructions for the day's work and left them to get on with it, which they did, even with some pride. On one occasion, Jim, Michael's work partner, returned from a visit and brought some disturbing news.

'Michael, you used to work for the Drapers up by Ballysteel, near Derry, did you not? Well, there was a tragedy there. Old Tom Draper was killed in an accident with his tractor. I have just heard but it was twelve months ago. I believe Mrs Draper, who was never much good, had left poor Tom some time before the accident. Nobody knows where she is.'

Michael was sorry about Tom because, in his own way, he had been good to him. He remembered Tom had taught him to drive and had quite often let him drive his tractor, which Michael had loved to do, but he also remembered how he had felt uncomfortable about his relationship with Elsie and how he had feared one day Tom would find out and also how Elsie would never leave him alone which was why he had moved on. Some days later, after another visit, Jim added some more about the Drapers.

'There was a three-year-old child, a boy, who the mother had not taken with her when she left. Tom cared for the boy although it was commonly thought that it was not his child. Anyhow, Tom's son by his first wife refused to acknowledge the child and the child is now in a children's home.'

The news was a bombshell to Michael. He suddenly knew that this child was his son. He was quite sure. Once or twice it had occurred to him that there might have been a child but when solid Tom was there he had not allowed himself to enquire because he felt he was in no position to take on the responsibility of fatherhood. Better to grow up as the child of a well-to-do farmer, as Tom was, than the offspring of a casual farm hand. But now it was all quite different. Tom was dead and the no-good mother had abandoned the little boy. Nobody knew where she was, Tom's family did not want the child and worse still they had put him into care.

Desperately, Michael said to Jim, 'Tell me about the boy.'

'I am afraid I don't know much more. I do remember the wife was quite upset about it. She said she always knew that Elsie Draper was a fast one but she did not know how anybody could go off and leave a child like that.'

Michael was no longer listening. Suddenly there rose in him the feeling of love so strong that it took possession of him. He never questioned why this should be. He simply knew that this child was his hope for the future, that this son gave him a purpose to his life and that he was part of himself. Then he realised the boy was in care. So many of his fellow prisoners had been in care. My God! This was something that must not happen to Robert, as the little boy was called.

'But it has happened and I am in prison and can do absolutely nothing about it.'

Michael returned to his wing and as time passed he could think of nothing else but Robert, the little boy he had deserted to grow up in a children's home, fed, housed, clothed, even educated, but unloved. Nobody to care whether he did well or not, so like himself and so many of his fellow inmates here.

For the next few days, and nights, he thought of little Robert. He thought of himself as a small child who did not belong to anybody, who had drifted from babyhood into a small, shy boy, to a teenager, desperately trying to penetrate into groups or gangs at school because, he recalled, he so much wanted to belong.

Then, with shame, he remembered stealing at the markets. His time at the training school. Happier times at Draper's Farm. His affair with Elsie. He hated Elsie. He hated himself. He despised his own weakness. Then he remembered the Robinsons. Edward – there was something about him that demanded respect: upright, gentlemanly, firm but with a twinkle in his eye. He could not imagine Edward doing anything mean or underhand. He could almost hear his educated, melodious voice. From there he naturally thought of Louise – that gentle lady was somebody altogether special. He could not actually find the right words to describe her, even to himself. Once again he felt shame as he remembered that he had stolen money from her handbag. His guilt grew as he recalled the greed that had caused him to be caught up with Packy and how the priest had said to him, when he was still on remand, that it was indeed no thanks to him that he had not caused the deaths of dear knows how many people and what other destruction he could have been responsible for. My God! What a father for Robert.

If Tom Draper had not been killed the boy would have had a chance, but his no-good mother had deserted him and he, his real father, was not any better.

Michael's despair deepened and he did not know where or who to turn to. He could not sleep and he hardly cared about the plants which previously he had taken so much pride in. Sometimes he thought, Poor bloody plants and seedlings. If I don't water and give them stakes, they will wither and die. More failures – my fault again. So, when out in the gardens work party, he tended the young annuals and tomato plants methodically, but he was so steeped in despair that there was no joy or satisfaction.

The duty officer and other staff noticed Michael's changed bearing and wondered what was wrong. Hardly a 'Dear John' because it was known that he was single and had no visitors or received any mail. The officers watched and observed him carefully.

One day, the chief officer, a man not without compassion, asked Michael, 'Lad, what is wrong? Have you a problem?'

Michael replied, 'Aye, I do and I don't know what to do about it. It is becoming more than I can bear.'

'Well, perhaps the chaplain, a social worker or a member of the Board of Visitors might be able to help. Why don't you put in an application paper to see somebody? Here is a form. Let me know if you need any help filling it in.'

Michael took the form and he read and reread it again when alone in his cell. He just could not see how anybody could help. Sadly, he thought, not even Joe, whom he still missed, would have been able to come up with a solution. 'There is just nothing I can do.'

Nevertheless, he opted for the Probation Officer, who came to see Michael a few days later. The interview was very difficult. Raymond Black was young and enthusiastic, eager to help where he could. He listened attentively and tried to draw Michael out.

He gathered Michael had had an affair with his employer's wife and that he had felt badly about this and disloyal to Tom, the husband, so much so that he had left his job, which he had liked, because he could not handle the situation. He had not known that a child had been born; he had just not thought about that seriously. He had learnt about the boy quite by chance on hearing that Tom Draper had been killed in an accident, that Elsie, the mother, had left, abandoning the child who Tom had offered to give his name and that on Tom's death the little boy had been put into care. Tom's relations would have nothing to do with him because they knew Elsie had been promiscuous.

Michael was now quite sure that Robert was his son. He had an overwhelming desire to acknowledge him as his son, to know what was to become of him. Raymond Black, even with his enthusiasm, could not see how he could help. He felt, but did not say, that it would not benefit the boy to know that his father was serving a ten-year sentence for a terrorist crime, and he need not know this. Better for him to believe his father, a respected farmer, was dead. He felt Michael should let things take their own course, since he was in no position to do anything for the child.

This was a very sad case. Raymond doubted very much that Michael would accept this because, in his experience, short though it was, prisoners, once they got hold of an idea, having so much time for reflection, usually held onto them. He promised to consider Michael's story and come back to him.

'I accept that I have no claim on the boy, but please try to trace him,' said Michael.

Chapter Eight

That night Michael, having tossed and turned, finally fell into a troubled sleep and dreamt that he was in the Robinsons' house with Raymond. They were sitting in the yellow and white sitting room; the door opened and Louise came in holding a little boy's hand. He could not see the child's face very clearly, but it was a happy scene. The boy was chatting and laughing merrily.

Louise turned to Michael and said, 'Robert now lives with us and we love him dearly.'

Michael was about to take Robert's hand in his when the scene changed. The sitting room was now a prison cell. Robert was alone! He was sitting on a narrow bed. He had an adult body but a child's head with babyish features. He was looking down at a grenade in his hands, which were covered with blood, and he was sobbing as though his heart would break. Large tears were mingling with the blood on his hands. Here, Michael woke up to find he was crying and the tears were his.

Days passed.

Michael was weighed down with despair. He heard nothing from Raymond. Every night the same dream returned to him – Robert, happy with Louise, glowing with health; then the scene would change – Robert, partly man and partly baby boy, with bloodied hands, weeping alone in a prison cell. Michael would wake in horror.

An idea came to Michael. At first it was vague and ill-formed, but gradually became more and more clear. Then it seemed to be quite plausible. He knew what he must do. He would contact the Robinsons and ask them to befriend Robert and visit him, and secretly he hoped they would adopt or foster him. He knew that this was a wild dream and highly improbable. He could not even remember their exact address, although he could see them clearly in his mind's eye. He did not know if they were at the same address or indeed if they were still alive. How could he contact them and how could he persuade them to visit Robert?

There were so many negative aspects that he nearly lost hope and almost dropped the whole idea, and yet when he remembered the personalities of the Robinsons, particularly Louise, he thought that if only he could see her, he would easily persuade her to take Robert under her wing. Perhaps she would be happy to take Robert; after all, she had told Michael that she had lost a boy and was always sad that she had never had another child.

On and on ran his thoughts until he persuaded himself that the Robinsons would at the very least take an interest in Robert and that he would come to no harm. Their influence, he reasoned, would save Robert from becoming one of life's failures which was how he saw himself. How could he even get in touch with the Robinsons and how could he ask a gentle lady like Louise to come to a place like Magilligan and go through the process of being searched as security demanded? Then, how could he expect her to mix with the other visitors? Such things he could not even contemplate.

Raymond Black did make some enquiries and found the children's home where Robert, aged four and a half, was now being cared for. He was told that suitable foster parents had not been found. It was hoped that his mother might send for him or come to fetch him but as yet nothing had been heard of her. Robert was a lively four year old who presented no problems. There was no mention that Robert's father was other than Tom Draper, though relatives had absolutely refused to take care for the child. The house mother did not know anything about the mother or why she had abandoned him. Raymond felt there was no useful purpose to giving Michael details of Robert's whereabouts seeing he had no legitimate claim on the child. Therefore, he was evasive when Michael finally approached him.

It became clear to Michael that if he was to trace Robert he would have to try another tactic. He decided to ask Jim, his fellow gardener, who had originally brought him the news of Tom Draper's death.

When they were alone in the greenhouse he asked, as casually as he could, if Jim had any further news of Elsie Draper. Had she sent for the boy?

Jim said, 'I do not really know, but at my next visit, which will be on the day after tomorrow, I will make some more enquiries about the family.' He added, 'I am really quite pleased to have a topic of conversation because believe it or not, the missus and I kind of run out of things to talk about after a bit. She is a good sort and does not make a poor mouth to me, and I know it is not easy for her with me in here and the kids and all.'

Michael thanked him and added, 'Ask her if she knows where the kid is being cared for. I should like to make a toy for him, poor little blighter.'

After his next visit Jim reported, 'The missus thought the boy was at Hollytree children's home in County Derry, and as far as she knew there was no word from the mother.'

This news gave Michael new hope and deep down he decided somehow he would contact the Robinsons and he would ask them to visit Robert. He had a feeling that they would take care of him, perhaps foster him or even adopt him. He realised this was an extremely far-fetched idea, almost an impossibility, but against all the odds the idea was firmly implanted and stayed with him as a secret hope to be treasured.

Michael calculated he must get in touch with the Robinsons. He thought about this and decided that the Church of Ireland chaplain would be his best bet. It was not difficult to have a few private words with the chaplain.

Although he was officially recorded as a Roman Catholic, he did not go to Mass on Sundays. He explained, 'I would like to write to Mr and Mrs Robinson. Would you kindly check their address?' He added, 'They lent me some money and now I would like to pay them back because they were good to me.'

The chaplain guessed that Michael had probably stolen and not borrowed money, but he decided to overlook this and give Michael the benefit of the doubt. 'I will consider this for you, Michael.'

He had a few words with the chief officer and was told, 'Michael Duffy is almost a model prisoner. I can see no reason why he should not write to these people. As far as I know he has no family. He certainly gets no visits nor does he receive any letters or send any out. We have noticed, of late, he does seem to have something on his mind. He is definitely worried about something.' As an afterthought the officer added, 'Anything he sends out will be censored, so there will be no chance of blackmail or other untoward requests.'

The Reverend Taylor made a number of telephone calls and fortunately one of his colleagues did know the Robinson family. 'They were a very nice couple, not very regular churchgoers, but I did see them from time to time. I could usually rely on Mrs Robinson's help with sales of work and other fund-raising events. They have two grown-up daughters and several grandchildren.'

So now Michael had the Robinsons' address. He set about writing to them. After many attempts he finally wrote a very short, simple letter asking them to visit him. He added that he needed advice about his son. He included a request for a visiting permit in the letter, adding that he was looking forward to seeing them, and he thanked them most sincerely. He handed the letter to be posted out, the first he had written since he had been in prison and one of the very few he had ever written in all his life.

Chapter Nine

Louise picked up the post at about ten o'clock ten days later. As was her custom, she sorted the letters; those for Edward and those for herself and also those addressed to Mr and Mrs Robinson. She then made the morning coffee and took the tray into the conservatory. One from Anne, her daughter in London, one from the local Red Cross and one to both of them in a buff envelope stamped 'On Her Majesty's Service.'

'What could this be?'

'Well open it and see. Best way to find out.'

Louise read and reread the letter and handed it to Edward, who immediately exclaimed, 'Well, of all the cheek! I suppose he wants money. Are there not numerous charities and statutory organisations to take care of this sort of thing? Throw that away. We certainly are not going to visit any criminal. Perhaps we had better write and tell him so.'

Louise said nothing, but she folded the letter away and intended to read it again when Edward was back in the garden. This she did, several times, and tried to picture Michael. She remembered him quite well and felt both shocked and sorry to learn that he was in prison. She had never known anybody who was or had been in prison.

The mention of Michael's son touched something in her, so she knew that whatever Edward said, she would have to go and see what it was all about. Surely Michael's son must be very young, little more than a baby. She said nothing to Edward but filled in the form requesting a visit permit and posted it off. She looked up exactly where Magilligan was on the road map. A week later she received the visiting permit and a list of regulations for visitors to Magilligan. The time allotted to them was from 11 a.m. to 12 noon on Wednesdays. They could visit once a week.

Edward had only once mentioned Michael's letter, but then at breakfast one morning he said, 'Have you written to that fellow in prison yet?'

Louise said, 'Actually, yes, I have written and I intend to go and see Michael, and what is more I hope you will come with me, but I am going anyway. There is a child involved.'

'I have far better things to do with my time, and I am sure you do too, than visiting fellows in prison,' muttered Edward.

However Louise was pleased and relieved. One day, Edward said, 'If you are determined to go on this wild goose chase I had better go along with you. If I was not retired now I would not have been able to get away and that would have been that.'

On the following Wednesday they set off for Magilligan, a drive of about twenty-five miles. They arrived in good time. There was no need to make enquiries; the visitors' car park and entrance were clearly marked. On ringing the bell in the high wire fence the gate was opened and a uniformed officer demanded to see their passes. These were exchanged for another set. Edward and Louise were directed along a passageway between high wire fences which loomed almost twenty feet above them.

On arriving at the reception area they were asked to hand over any parcels they had brought. Louise had brought sweets and fruit. They were further directed to separate searching booths. Louise felt the atmosphere was austere to the extreme, not improved by the overall shabby nature of the waiting area.

When Louise's turn came to be searched she was beckoned to a small cubicle where two female searchers, calling
her 'dear', asked to see the contents of her handbag, which
they went through with extreme thoroughness, followed by
a brief body search which included taking off her shoes.

'Not been here before, dear?' said one lady.

'It is just our job you know,' said the other. 'That is all
now. Just wait until you are called.'

Louise then joined Edward in yet another waiting room
with wooden benches around the walls, peeling paint and a
few notices pinned up with information considered of
interest to visitors. Also there was some graffiti.

'This beats even the worst railway stations,' Edward said,
with a smile.

Another wait and then they were called. 'Mr and Mrs
Robinson, please take table number six.'

So they went into the large visiting hall and made their
way to table number six. There were several visits in
progress. While they waited, they looked around the large,
pleasant hall, quite different from the approaches. At one
end there was a raised dais where three officers sat. In one
corner there was a play area with a video showing a cartoon;
several boys and girls watched intently, sitting on pint-sized
chairs. A few more were busy drawing or playing with a
variety of toys at play tables. The Robinsons noted the
attractive pictures on the walls and pot plants in jardinieres
at intervals around the hall. Louise thought the flowers did
not look particularly healthy and badly needed watering.

They both noted the rather sharp contrast between the
prisoners and their visitors. The former were mostly young,
healthy-looking men in freshly laundered casual wear while
their women folk looked to be poorly dressed, though
many were heavily made up with elaborate hairdos. They
sat facing each other, some holding hands.

Edward noticed that at the furthest end of the room there was a small window in the wall, high above the heads of everyone, which he rightly supposed was yet another observation position. The tables were spaced well apart so that conversations would not be overheard but every move could be seen by the officers.

Nevertheless, both Edward and Louise thought the overall atmosphere was pleasant and even welcoming, and those having visits were relaxed, in contrast to Louise who was tense and nervous, unnerved by this first experience of prison. She was altogether unprepared to see the children. She had never realised that children would be visiting, but of course they would want to come and see their fathers and the fathers would want to see their children, and maybe there was no one at home to look after them while their mothers were away.

Louise was thinking how sad it was for families, when Michael came and sat opposite them. She sensed that Edward was uneasy.

After what seemed to be a long silence, he put out his hand to Louise and said, 'It was very good of you to come. Thank you very much, ma'am.'

Louise smiled and said, 'How are you, Michael?'

Before he could answer Edward said, 'What is your particular problem? How do you think we can help you?' At this point a pleasant young woman came alongside their table with a tea trolley, asking if they would like tea or coffee at twenty pence per cup. Biscuits and chocolate bars were also on offer.

This provided a welcome interlude and gave Michael time to sort out his well-prepared story. Slowly, in a small voice, he told them that he believed that he had a son, aged four years, called Robert. Looking at Edward and Louise, his own story seemed very shameful. He was afraid that they might get up and leave, but they listened to everything he told them.

Michael shifted in his chair and crumbled his biscuits as he explained how he was so unhappy that his son was going to be brought up in care. He said, 'I know, from my own experience and from what so many of the prisoners here tell me, that although we were well looked after, nobody really cared much about us, whether we did well at school or what we did or thought. There were always so many different people looking after us there was nobody to get really fond of.' He paused. 'I just don't know why, but suddenly knowing that I have a son has changed my life. I desperately want my boy to have a better chance in life than I had.'

Edward was very serious and said, 'Am I to believe that you think you have ended up here because you were orphaned? Come on, my boy! You cannot blame those who tried to look after you.'

Michael said, weakly, 'Never mind me, sir. I just want my son, as I said, to have a better chance in life than I have had. Will you please visit him at the children's home and see for me that the foster parents he is sent to will be good to him?'

It was all out now and Michael felt relieved. Before Edward had time to say yes or no, Louise said, 'Michael, we will visit Robert for you,' and as she said this, she smiled. From there the visit became easier.

Questions and answers were exchanged concerning the prison routine. Michael told them what he thought they would like to hear. He told them he worked in the prison gardens because he felt Louise would be interested. He also told them he did a fair amount of drawing and painting, some during working hours, and how helpful the art mistress was, so much so that he did a lot of his work in his spare time.

Mrs Moore was a wonderful person and teacher who had helped him and encouraged him to take up and keep up many forms of art, including advising him on his reading. 'There is a good library for prisoners,' he added.

He did not tell them about his fellow prisoners who divided themselves into two very distinct groups, one Catholic and nationalist and the other Protestant and loyalist, or that they were very bigoted and coarse when untroubled and undisturbed and could become violent in the extreme when roused by anything they deemed to be an injustice. Nor did he tell them about the continual background noises of raised voices and the clanging of heavy doors and gates being locked and unlocked. Again, he did not mention the indignity of their persons being searched, also their cells, when every single possession was turned over and pulled about. He did not mention the long, lonely hours locked away in the cells and the appalling practice of slopping out, that some men were unable to cope and were overcome by despair and attempted suicide, that two men had hanged themselves in the past year.

He told them that he had another six years to serve. He did not expect to lose any remission as he had managed to stay out of trouble, as he put it. So, it might not be quite so long. He added that if it were not for his worry about Robert, which now was with him day and night, his life inside was tolerable.

'Another dreadful thing is,' he said, 'I stole ten pounds from you on that day when you had that fall. It fell out of your handbag and I pocketed it. I would like to arrange to pay you back. I have earned some cash in here, so I can arrange for it to be sent to you. I can't hand it over in here; we are not allowed to actually handle money, but there is a system whereby our money is recorded so that we can't use it for betting and gambling.'

Louise was about to tell him not to worry when Edward said, 'Very good, Michael. Just do that.'

Louise said, 'I have left a parcel for you. I hope it gets to you.'

They shook hands and departed their separate ways. Michael felt calmer and happy enough about the outcome of the visit. It had been better than he had dared to hope for. Louise felt full of compassion for Michael because to her he had appeared to be very dispirited. He seemed somehow different from the other prisoners she saw who, on the whole, were very cheerful and not too unhappy with their lot.

Edward was inclined to feel anger that he had allowed himself to be involved. After all, he thought, the chap is serving a long sentence. His crime must have been serious.

Michael had not actually told them about his offence, trial and conviction, and they had not asked. However, all that had nothing to do with the child.

Edward found himself thinking, Poor child. Deserted by his mother, and his father in prison, at best a weak character. What a mess. Then he thought, I will visit that young man without Louise and get him to tell me all the details. We cannot go ahead until we are fully aware of all the facts.

Louise and Edward said little to each other on the way home. The visit had been traumatic for both of them. Michael had been cagey about what went on behind those high wire fences and walls. He did appear to be genuinely concerned about the child. Pity he had not thought about him, poor little thing, before he had got himself into trouble.

Chapter Ten

Exactly two weeks after their visit to Magilligan, Edward and Louise drove to Hollytree Children's Home at 4 p.m. because they had been informed at that time that all the children were back from their respective schools although Robert, being still only four, was back at the home earlier.

On their arrival a house mother welcomed them, saying, 'I am so pleased for Robert to have visitors.' She added, 'Perhaps if this visit goes well, Mr and Mrs Robinson, you might befriend him and occasionally take him out for a treat. Would you like some tea before you meet Robert? He is a dear little boy. No trouble at all.'

Edward marvelled at the way tea always seemed to be served at awkward moments in life. Afterwards they were shown into a large, bright play room where a group of children were watching TV. None of the children moved or turned round as they entered.

Mrs Leeson pointed Robert out to them. He was the smallest of the group, a solid, fair-haired little boy. As his name was called out he turned round for a split second and then continued to stare at the television, sitting erect, mouth slightly open, podgy hands on his knees, as if drawn by an invisible magnet to the flickering screen.

Edward saw an amazing likeness to Michael. There could be no doubt that this was Michael Duffy's son.

Louise and Mrs Leeson went over to Robert and tried, not too successfully, to draw him away from the television. 'How are you, Robert?' asked Louise.

'I am watching television,' came the reply.

Again Louise tried. 'How old are you, Robert?'

'I am ten,' came the immediate reply.

'You are not. You are only four,' all the other children chanted.

'Honest, he is only four and still goes to play school,' said a little girl of about six or seven.

'Anybody like a toffee?' Louise tried once again. This was better than TV and everybody turned round, hands in the air, ready to take a toffee and hoping to be offered another.

'Did I hear anybody say "thank you" to Mrs Robinson?' asked Mrs Leeson. 'Now, children, say 'thank you' and then go and get your milk or juice. That is all except Robert. Mr and Mrs Robinson want to have a little chat with him.'

As they left, the little girl, called Sally, piped up, 'He tells terrible lies and he wets the bed most nights.'

Robert turned a little pink and screwed up his face as if to cry and then changed his mind, bent over and firmly planted his teeth into Sally's shoulder. Sally let out a piercing scream.

'Serve her right,' someone said. Turning to Mrs Leeson, he added, 'It ain't nice to tell tales, is it?'

Mrs Leeson tut-tutted and told the children to hurry off to the canteen and get their drinks, all except Robert. Robert was now looking quite pleased with himself.

'Do you often bite your friends, Robert?'

'They are not my friends. They are just children.' The subject was then dropped. It was felt the less attention Robert got from biting, the better.

Mrs Leeson asked, 'Would you like to visit Mr and Mrs Robinson and have tea with them, Robert?'

'Have they got a TV?'

'I am sure they do.'

'Have they got a big car?'

And so it was arranged that Robert should go out with the Robinsons to tea on the following Saturday. Before they left, Mrs Leeson asked, 'Would you like to see Robert's social worker and learn a little of his background?'

This was tentatively arranged for the following Wednesday when she was expected to call at the home. Robert would be at play school. Even before they left Hollytree Louise felt a surge of love for Robert. She saw that the home was quite nice and that somebody had tried to make it as attractive as possible for these poor children without parents to give them a home. Mrs Leeson seemed a kind person.

Then she remembered Michael saying how nobody cared individually for children in care and she understood how that could happen. They were cared for but not especially loved, and little children needed to be loved just as much as they needed a bed, their food and education. She was filled with compassion for all the children at Hollytree but it was already love that she felt for Robert.

On the way home she said to Edward, 'Robert has a strong resemblance to Michael. Did you see it? I think he is a dear little boy. What did you think?'

'He seems a nice fellow, poor little chap. I am afraid he does not have a very bright future. You only have to look at his background.'

'Oh Edward! We must befriend him, as that Mrs Leeson said. I quite look forward to taking him out and giving him treats.'

'Hold on. We must not get too involved. It is all very well dealing with a charming four year old, but I am afraid there may be bad blood there.'

Louise said nothing. She was already planning the kind of treats she would give Robert. She only hoped that he would not be too shy and that he would take to them.

Would she be able to manage him? She thought she would cope at least for an afternoon at a time; after all, he was only four and Mary's children were quite good when they were with her.

They returned home and continued to have mixed and troubled feelings. Louise had no doubts that she must help Robert. Somehow they must get him away from his background and set him on a better course for his future. Such a lovely child – he must not grow up to be a failure or, worse still, a criminal.

Edward said, 'In spite of everything, I am strongly drawn to this child, but my head warns me of becoming involved with him and especially with his father. We could be in very deep waters there.'

When Edward and Louise finally met Robert's social worker she told them much that they already knew. She also added, 'Robert has settled very well and is an uncomplicated child with few problems. Considering that his family life has been totally disrupted, one would have expected behavioural problems but this is not the case, beyond occasional bed-wetting.'

She asked if they knew that Mr Draper was almost certainly not the boy's father but had allowed the boy to take his name, although the birth had never been registered, for some reason.

'We are informed,' she continued, 'that Elsie Draper was unashamedly promiscuous. After Tom Draper's death the family would take no responsibility either for Elsie or her child. It is not clear why or when she left or her exact whereabouts. She was in London and may or may not be there still. At first it was hoped that she might come and collect Robert, not that she is a suitable person to bring up a child. Anyhow, nothing has been heard of her, so in the meanwhile we, in the Children's Department, will try and find a suitable foster home for him.' She continued, 'If you,

Mr and Mrs Robinson, are good enough to take an interest in Robert and take him out on a regular basis and make him feel wanted and to have people who care for him, it would be the most wonderful thing for him.'

While they both knew that they were getting themselves into a situation fraught with problems and although they had made no promises to Michael, in their hearts they both knew that they could not fail Robert. Instinctively, they both knew that sooner or later they were going to take Robert into their home.

Anne, their unmarried daughter, clearly foresaw enormous difficulties and would have liked to have saved her parents from what she saw as a very great folly, but she also realised it would be useless to try to dissuade her mother to give up the idea.

'I suppose you think you can adopt Robert?'

'No, we know we cannot do that. His mother is still alive and in any case we are too old, but what we can do and may do is to take him as a foster child. As such, we will get professional help and advice if and when we require it with any problems and for mapping out his future. We will have advice at the highest level.'

'I think you are both quite mad,' said Anne. She got up and kissed her mother, saying, 'For what it is worth, Mum and Dad, I will be behind you in your madness. Perhaps you won't be good enough to be foster parents,' she added with a grin. 'It will interesting to see, in years to come, whether breeding or environment are the stronger force.'

To her surprise, her mother's eyes filled up with tears as Louise sobbed, 'I could not bear Robert to end up in that place.'

Robert spent several Saturdays with the Robinsons. He appeared to be amazingly self-confident. He enjoyed being driven in the car. He chatted away about the other children in the home and at his play school. He also told them some fantastic tales about places he had visited and things he had seen and done. He watched TV and ate most of the meals Louise most carefully prepared for him.

'Can I take back some of the things I can't finish in case I get hungry?' asked Robert.

Louise explained, 'Leftovers would not be very nice by the time you get back but I will give you a little package to take back of things that will not spoil.' Robert settled for that.

One day they had a picnic by the sea. Robert was completely overwhelmed with delight and wanted to bring back not only shells but also sand. Louise made a mental note that they would have to make a sandpit in the garden.

When she suggested this to Edward, he said, 'Don't you think you are jumping over your fences before you come to them? Sand pits will be the least of our problems.'

Each time Robert returned to the home he waved. 'Goodbye. See you next Saturday.'

Edward always hoped that a good foster home would be found and that Robert would settle into a good environment. They would keep in touch and visit him and even take him out for treats. He understood that the Children's Department encouraged such arrangements.

Louise found herself becoming more and more attached to Robert and she dreaded the thought of him being moved away. She constantly thought about him. She knew she should not become so involved, but she simply could not help herself. She kept seeing him sitting in front of the TV or sitting up at the kitchen table on a cushion, enjoying his lunch or tea with relish. At times she saw a likeness to James and thought perhaps Robert was sent to them as a replacement for James. She knew she could not lose Robert.

Edward and Louise had only once communicated with Michael; this was when Edward wrote saying that they had seen Robert and that he was well and seemed happy at present in a small children's home. He also said that it was expected that fairly soon a suitable foster home would be found, but they would keep in touch with him.

One weekend Mary, the married daughter, came with her three children and her husband, Bill, from County Wicklow to spend a few days. Mary, a former nurse, was an easygoing person, totally involved with her family and their life on the farm in Wicklow. She did not know anything about Robert. Somehow it had never come up, and now Louise wondered if they should have Robert as usual on this Saturday.

She decided he could not be disappointed so, when the family arrived, Robert had already been collected. There was no time before lunch to explain who he was. It was only afterwards, over coffee, when the older children were in the garden, that Louise explained that this was an orphan she and Edward were interested in and who usually spent Saturdays with them.

Mary accepted this, adding, 'He seems a nice little fellow and I hope the afternoon will pass off without anyone getting beaten up.'

She knew only too well that her family were not above having a good free-for-all, but she expected that Robert, coming from a children's home, could probably stand up for himself. In the event the children did get on well, playing football and climbing trees.

When it was time for Robert to go back, he said to Louise, 'I like your children, but I really like it better when they aren't here as then it is just me. I like that. I hope they don't come any more Saturdays. Saturdays are my days. Promise.'

Louise was somewhat nonplussed, but Mary said, 'Don't worry, Mum. Kids are selfish little beings. He does not mean it.'

Mary dismissed the incident, usually preoccupied with the needs of her husband and children, and did not give too much thought to Robert. However, that night, before going to sleep, she suddenly thought about the little boy and she also remembered James, the little brother who had been killed, and it did occur to her that her parents, especially her mother, did appear to be very fond of the child. They had always been very loving parents and grandparents. She was not altogether surprised that they had befriended a little orphan.

Next day, Penny, her five-year-old daughter, asked if Robert would be coming again because she liked him. He was quite nice, for a boy, and he was near to her age. Mary then realised that Robert was becoming important to her parents. Little did she guess just how important.

Soon after the family had returned home, Edward approached the Children's Department of the Health and Social Services Board and requested that he and his wife wished their names to be considered as foster parents for the little boy known as Robert Draper. They expected to have some opposition on account of their age, and so were very pleased, and a little surprised, when the formalities were completed with the minimum delay and they received notification that they could take Robert into their home as a foster child. He would continue to be the responsibility of the Children's Department but this simply meant that his social worker would visit from time to time. Also, she would be on hand to advise should there be any problems. They would receive an allowance towards the expenses of keeping and caring for Robert.

Chapter Eleven

When Edward arrived to collect Robert from the children's home, the little boy was waiting for him in Mrs Leeson's office, with his small suitcase and a paper carrier bag with a few toys.

He very calmly said goodbye to Mrs Leeson, took Edward's hand and waved as they drove away. On arrival at the house in the Limavady Road, once in the hall, he took off his coat and, standing squarely, looking at Louise, said, 'I have come. When is tea?'

At bedtime he climbed into bed, pulled up the duvet, smiled at Louise, put two fingers in his mouth and was almost immediately asleep.

Next morning at about seven he appeared round the master bedroom door and climbed into bed beside Edward and Louise. After a minute or two he got out and came back with a book which he pushed into Louise's face saying, 'Read,' which she proceeded to do.

When the book was finished Louise said, 'I am now going to make us some tea. Would you like some milk or juice?'

While Louise was away Robert thrust the book towards Edward. 'Read,' he said.

'Don't you say anything else, old chap?' said Edward, sleepily.

When Louise returned with the tray Robert took his juice and when this was finished, he once again said, 'Read.'

Louise said, 'Not now. It is getting-up time. Would you like some breakfast?'

Robert spent his first few days following either Edward or Louise about like a small pet dog, saying very little. After about a week he suddenly announced, 'I like it here. I am never going back to Hollytree.'

Then he added, 'I think I might go back once because I left my special *Thomas the Tank Engine* book there and I don't want them to have it. When can we go and get it?'

Edward bought a replacement book and Robert never mentioned the home again.

Shortly after this, Robert started school. He settled down well and was always eager to go every morning. Satisfactory reports came back from his teacher. Soon the kitchen walls were decorated with drawings and brightly coloured paintings which Robert brought almost every day.

Although he was obviously happy at school, he would never tell Louise or Edward what he did. When asked he would smile and say, 'I forget' or, 'I will tell you tomorrow.'

Once Robert asked Louise, 'Why have I not got a mummy and daddy like the children at school?'

Before Louise could think how to answer this, Robert said, 'I don't need any but you,' and then he added, 'I am going to call you Lou and Edward Da and I like it here. I like being the only child in the house, because I have you, all to myself. I think that is quite lucky, don't you think it is, having only me? Could we have a dog? I would love to have a dog – a big dog. I would have a red collar for him and a shiny dish for his food and we could all go for lovely walks.' Edward said they would have to think about this.

Over the next four years the Robinsons marvelled at the way Robert had settled with them, and also at school where he was happy and progressing well. He was a happy, sunny-natured little boy who was well adjusted and who had no behavioural problems.

One day, not long after he came to live with the Robinsons, he said he had a friend called Charlie Brown and would they like to get to know him. He turned round, beckoned and said, 'Come on, Charlie Brown. This is Lou and this is Da.'

It was some time before Louise realised that 'Charlie Brown' was an imaginary character who had followed Robert like a shadow for at least two years. Robert could often be heard talking to his imaginary friend.

At other times, when given a sweet, he would say, 'Please can I have one for Charlie Brown?'

Louise soon became adept at coping with Charlie Brown, who was sometimes blamed for small misdemeanours, but on the whole neither Edward nor Louise were caused any serious problems by Robert or his friend.

One day, Edward brought a Labrador puppy and suddenly Charlie Brown disappeared. The puppy was called Folly and she caused considerable disruption in the house, continually picking up shoes, gloves, hats or anything within reach. Some of these she chewed up and others hid away in odd places. A few items were never found. She was not above stealing from the table and worktops, all of which caused Robert to shriek with laughter. He would say that Folly was only a puppy and did not know any better.

Folly grew large and handsome and became Robert's devoted friend. Gradually she became calmer and more biddable. Robert was encouraged to feed her and take some responsibility for her by playing ball with her in the garden to get rid of some of her surplus energy and to brush her glossy black coat, an exercise they both enjoyed. When Robert was not at school they were inseparable.

Unbeknown to Robert, Edward and Louise kept in contact with Michael. They usually visited him once a month, sometimes together, and occasionally Edward went without Louise. The visits passed off easily. Michael was avid for news of Robert, eager to see photographs and hear every possible detail of his day-to-day progress.

When alone with Michael, Edward made Michael promise that he would not disclose his true relationship to Robert until such time as it was considered that Robert could cope with the fact that his father was in prison. At this time Robert believed that his father was dead. This was painful and difficult for Michael to accept but he gave his solemn word.

Edward and Louise lived with the constant worry that one day Robert's mother would return and try to take him away from them. As the years passed and there was no word from Elsie, another and more pressing anxiety kept haunting them – soon Michael would be released from prison and would most certainly want to see Robert and even make himself known to him, even though he had promised he would not claim any right to the boy.

'Because,' as he frankly said to Edward, 'I am now happy for Robert. I know I could not hope to be a father to him.'

Edward worried that he might not be able to keep his word, and if he did go back on his promise, how would Robert feel if he knew his father was a convicted terrorist?

The Robinsons had been advised to allow Robert to think his father was dead. It had been bad enough telling him that his mother had abandoned him. There had been no easy way of camouflaging this.

Robert had accepted that his mother had not been able to take him with her when she went away. He never asked why this should have been until one day, when he was about six, he suddenly asked, 'Why did my mother not like me?' adding, 'I am glad she did not take me with her to wherever she went because I hate her and I only love you and Da and nobody else.'

Again, he said, as he had said once before, 'I like being the only child in the house because I don't have to share you with anybody except Folly and she is a dog and that is all right. I don't mind the grandchildren because they are quite nice and they are not here very often. I do like it when we go down to see them on their farm. I think I might be a farmer when I grow up.'

Louise was rather taken back by the strong conviction behind Robert's pronouncement about his mother, and although she was touched by his declaration of love, she did wonder if somehow she should have defended his mother's character. On balance, she thought, it was better not to labour the point. She sincerely hoped she had not taken the coward's way out. Many times over both the Robinsons wondered if it was morally right to deceive Robert about his father.

Their daughters, Mary and Anne, knew all about Robert from before the time he had actually come to live with their parents and they felt that if it made Edward and Louise happy to foster a child, it was a good thing, especially as they had lost James, even though that was so long ago.

When they were asked whether Robert should be told about his real father, they both thought it was probably wiser to wait until he was older, and only then if they felt he could cope with such a revelation.

Siobhan, Robert's social worker, who became a family friend and welcome visitor, was of the same opinion. So the question of Robert's origins was never discussed.

When Robert first came to stay with the Robinsons, some of their friends did wonder who the little boy was. Louise and Edward merely said he was an orphan who was now a member of the family; very soon he was accepted as such and nobody ever thought of him as anything but a member of the Robinson family.

Chapter Twelve

Williams & Harris
Solicitors & Commissioners for Oaths
30 Swan Street
Perth
West Australia

3rd December, 1979

To the Children's Department
Londonderry
North of Ireland

Dear Sir,

My client, who for the present does not wish me to disclose her name or address, has asked me to enquire about the welfare of her son, Robert Draper, born 3/12/1971 in Londonderry. She wishes to be informed if he is in need of anything and if he is being cared for.

We will be grateful if you can forward this information for us to pass onto our client.

Thank you,
Yours truly,

George Harris

As William Glen, head of the Children's Department, read this letter, he remembered that Siobhan McNutt was the social worker in charge of the Draper child. He sent a message for her to come and bring Robert's file.

'Ah, Siobhan. Come in and read this letter while I have a look at Robert's file.'

'I do hope Robert's mother is not going to come and take Robert away!' exclaimed Siobhan. 'He is so wonderfully settled with the Robinsons. They are such very nice people and good foster parents. It would be a tragedy if he was moved away from such a good home.'

'Well, my guess is that the mother is having a touch of conscience about the boy. I see she left him when he was only six weeks old and has not been in contact since. I think she will be happy enough to leave him with his foster parents but, just in case, I will have him made a ward of court. That will give us time to find out about her character and present situation. From all accounts she was not a very suitable or good mother. Mind you, if she were to come and claim him it would be very difficult and eventually she might be allowed to take the boy with her. I will not send any information until I have her name, as she may be remarried, and her address, so that we can make our enquiries.'

William made an appointment to visit the Robinsons and to see Robert and after this he was quite sure it would be in Robert's best interest to remain in their care. He thought, If only more cases of fostering were as successful, there would be many fewer problem children. I must pull out all the stops to keep the boy where he is. I suppose the Robinsons are too old to adopt, but the mother need not know that.

He sent a letter demanding all of Elsie's particulars. When these finally arrived he learnt Elsie was remarried and only wished to be reassured about Robert's welfare. He sent off a long and detailed report on Robert and enquired if Elsie would consider allowing the present foster parents to adopt Robert. He knew this was highly irregular but thought it was worth trying, and as it turned out a reply came back saying that Elsie was willing to agree to this as she only had the boy's welfare in mind.

William discussed this with his senior colleagues and they agreed that it would be unproductive to pursue the question of adoption any further because the Robinsons would be turned down because of their age and the process would be painful for them. It had been successful in as much as now Elsie would be unlikely to make any claims on the boy. Maybe she was genuine in that she only wanted what was best for Robert.

William had not given Robert's address to Elsie or her solicitor, so that she would be unable to contact or trouble them by going to them directly. William was quite pleased with the outcome because, although there was no absolute guarantee, it could be hoped that Robert would be safe with the Robinsons for the foreseeable future.

When Louise and Edward learnt all that had gone on they were both grateful and relieved. Edward said that some time later, when Robert would have to know about his mother, he could decide for himself if he wished to make contact.

He said, 'He is going to face some unpalatable revelations.'

Michael, in prison, thought a great deal about Robert. Sometimes he would fantasise about being united with him after his release. Then common sense would tell him that he could never do for Robert what the Robinsons were doing for him, and although he was happy about the way things were working out, he did experience a terrible sadness at the thought of never being able to acknowledge his son.

At other times he felt a deep bitterness at his own sheer stupidity to have allowed himself to be duped by Packy Coyle. When tormented with these feelings, usually when alone in his cell, he could calm himself by looking at the photographs he had of Robert: a chubby four year old laughing into the camera and later a serious six year old and a bigger boy with a faint smile, looking straight at him as though to reassure him that all was well and not to worry.

Michael would say to himself, 'I don't want anything except that Robert will have a better start in life than I had and I could not ask for more than he now has. I have made a solemn promise which I must keep.'

Sometimes, a small voice would say to him, 'You only promised not to reveal yourself to Robert until such time as they think he will not be too upset by knowing about you. Perhaps that time is not too far away.'

Michael knew in reality that this was a long way off, but it was not impossible and that was a comfort. He could only hope that Robert would not reject him. No good going on like this. He must make an enormous effort to get a grip on himself. He would then get out his drawing and painting materials and set to work. This usually absorbed him and after an hour or so he would become calm and quite unagitated.

He loved this work and he wondered what would have become of him if he had not taken the art classes or had Mrs Moore to advise and guide him. He would do a picture for Robert of his dog. He would have to find a picture of a black Labrador to copy, even though all black dogs were difficult to paint.

Chapter Thirteen

Once, when Edward and Louise were visiting Michael together, he said, 'This year I am hoping to get Christmas parole. If I do, would it be possible for me to see Robert, even for a few minutes? I have never seen him. I promise, faithfully, that I will keep my promise and not tell him that I am his father. I do so much want to see him. Could you arrange it? Please.'

'I will consider this and think about it and what would be best,' replied Edward. 'Are you quite sure that we can rely on you keeping your word not to tell Robert at present? We both know that Robert will most certainly have to learn the truth some time, but after very careful consideration we have decided that it is best for Robert and for you, Michael, if this is delayed until he is a little older and until you are back in the community making a fresh start, which will now not be so very far away. I personally will help you get on your feet again. So, you must be patient. I appreciate this is most difficult for you. Somehow, we will arrange for you to see Robert, if you get your parole, but if and only if you keep your side of the bargain.'

Michael readily agreed.

When they were on their way home after the visit, Edward expressed grave doubts about such a meeting taking place. 'How would it go? Could any good come of it? Would they both be hurt? It would be my guess that Michael would come out of it worse. Robert was not unduly upset about his mother having abandoned him. Mind you, he does not yet know that we now know where she is, but it will be much more difficult for Michael, because he cares so much and has no one else, really. He would have to bear his hurt alone, whereas we can soften the pain for Robert because we are with him and he does not even know Michael.'

Louise suggested that they invite Michael to spend Christmas Day with them. 'Mary, John and the children will be with us and Anne. We can say it is a Christian act to invite a stranger without a family to share our Christmas.'

Edward thought this might be plausible. When they next saw Michael they asked if he would be getting parole.

He answered, 'I hope so, but I can't be absolutely sure. If I do I will be staying at a hostel in Londonderry.'

When told about the plan for him to spend Christmas Day with them, he was quite overwhelmed. 'I can't thank you enough.'

So that Christmas Day, when all the family were together, the house bright with decorations of holly and ivy, presents piled under the tree and the children high with excitement, Louise called the children together and said, 'This Christmas we are inviting a stranger to join us for dinner, and I hope you will all make him very welcome.'

At about twelve thirty, Michael stood on the doorstep and timidly knocked on the door. He was trying very hard to conceal his emotion and finding it almost beyond him. The thought of actually seeing Robert and the wonderful kindness of Edward and Louise he knew would render him speechless when he got inside.

Edward opened the door. Smiling, he said, 'Come on in. Come on in. You are most welcome on this Christmas Day.'

The children crowded round the door chattering, and then together they chorused, 'Happy Christmas,' as they eyed Michael. 'Come and see our Christmas tree.'

Michael looked to see which child was Robert. He must be the older of the boys. That lovely blond boy with the ready smile. Even to himself Michael could not analyse his feelings, and he was thankful he did not have time for reflection as a tiny girl took his hand and led him to the tree.

She lisped, 'If what you have in your bag is presents, you must put them under the tree. Is there one for me?'

Penny, the eldest girl, briskly told her to shut up. At that moment Louise emerged, a little flushed, from the kitchen, saying, 'Happy Christmas, Michael. You are very welcome.'

Michael could only manage, 'Thank you.'

Dinner passed off well. Michael thought, I have never seen such a display of fine and beautiful china and silver, nor such food. A golden-brown turkey, carved by Edward, accompanied by mouth-watering vegetables and sauces.

When this was finished, everybody, except the smallest girl, carried plates and dishes into the kitchen and returned to their places. The lights were turned out leaving only the flickering fire light. The door opened and Louise appeared holding a dish, almost above her head, with a large plum pudding which appeared to be on fire, blue flames surrounding it.

Everybody clapped and shouted with one voice, 'Wish, wish before the flames go away. Hurry and make your wish.'

Michael was quite speechless, but with the overall excitement this went unnoticed except by Louise who once or twice met his eyes and smiled. When the crackers were pulled and the paper hats donned, only then was Michael able to study Robert.

98

His eyes filled with tears. He thought, I am glad, oh so glad, that my son is in the care of these good and kind people. Surely nothing bad can happen to him when he is part of this family?

When dinner was over Michael had recovered and was in control of his emotions sufficiently to insist on helping with the washing up and general clearing away. Shyly he said, 'I am quite good at this,' so they allowed him to help.

Before long Edward was standing at the door, saying, 'It is time for presents. Little Jane is nearly asleep and the boys and Penny are tired of waiting.'

Michael received two parcels which were soft and bulky. He handed over three large, flat parcels; one for Louise, one for Edward and one for Robert. He had also brought an outsized box of sweets for the whole family.

Robert opened his present from Michael to find a painting of a black Labrador. 'This is just like Folly. Oh, thank you. Did you do it yourself?'

'Yes I did. I like dogs, and I think you do too.'

By this time Louise and Edward had opened their presents; a delicately painted water colour of summer flowers for Louise and a study of swallows for Edward.

'How lovely, Michael,' said Louise. 'You are quite an artist. Your work is very good. Thank you.'

Penny then approached Michael. 'Could you please do me a picture of a pony. I don't have one of my own but I love ponies. I will have one soon, but I ride one called Minstrel; she is lovely. She is grey and has a white mane and tail and she has dark insides to her ears and black dapples on her back.'

Michael promised to take Penny's order. 'I will do my best to get her portrait right. I really don't know much about horses, but some of my friends do. I mostly know about cows.'

Henry, who was five, said, 'Do you know about tractors? I would love a picture of a tractor. I like tractors better than ponies.'

Everyone laughed, but Michael was pleased to have been asked to do something, he felt, in return for the hospitality he had received from the Robinson family.

When it was time for the younger children to go to bed and for Michael to say goodbye, Henry said, 'Goodbye, Michael. Don't forget about my picture of a tractor.'

Robert said, 'I really love my picture of Folly. Thank you very much.'

Edward walked out to the porch with Michael. 'Would you like me to drive you back to the hostel?'

'Oh no, thank you. I will walk. Thank you and please thanks Mrs Robinson. This has been a wonderful day for me.'

Edward said, 'All right. Robert, as you can see, is well and happy and doing well. When are you due back?'

'On the day after tomorrow.'

'I will drive you back and we can have a talk about your future. Goodnight, Michael. I will pick you up at the hostel at about ten thirty; I know where it is.'

Michael made his way back to the hostel with mixed feelings. It had been so good seeing Robert, but very hard not to make himself known to him. At the same time, he realised he had to do what the Robinsons advised about this.

He thought sadly, Perhaps Robert will never know who I am and what he means to me. After all, what can I ever do for him compared with what they are doing for him? Even after I get out I may never get a job again. He said he would help. I wonder if he can. Can anybody?

With these thoughts running through his head he reached the hostel. Some of the men were watching television.

'Hello, Mike. Had a good time with your posh friends? Lucky for some, although the nosh here was okay today.'

Michael decided to go to bed. He wanted to keep the memories of today and he hoped he would dream about his Christmas Day. He decided when he got back that he would paint some of the scenes he had just experienced, and of course he must not forget the kids' orders.

Next day he went to a football match with some of the residents at the hostel, and on the following morning he was ready when Edward drove up to bring him back to Magilligan. Anne, Edward's daughter, was with him.

'Jump in, Michael,' said Edward. 'Anne has come along to keep me company. She knows all about you so you need not worry about speaking freely. I want to discuss your future with you. You have only less than a year to serve.'

'That is right, sir. Do you think I will ever be able to get work? I will do anything, absolutely anything, but I would like to work on a farm or at least something out of doors.'

'I will try to think of something when the time comes,' said Edward. 'It won't be easy. I will make some enquiries on your behalf. Meanwhile, keep optimistic and work on the art – it might come in useful somewhere.'

'I will. I have applied for a pre-release course, which is said to be helpful, because I am quite out of touch, being inside for so long. I know I would not have survived without Mrs Robinson and you. I do thank you, from the bottom of my heart, especially for taking in and caring for Robert. He is very lucky.'

'They are too,' said Anne, 'because Robert is a super kid and he has been good for my parents. He is a pure joy for them.'

After this, all three were silent until they approached the Magilligan campus. Michael got out of the car.

He shook hands with Anne, who said cheerfully, 'Good luck, Michael. See you a free man in less than one year.

Not so long now and don't forget the pictures for the kids – one grey pony and one tractor – colour not specified.'

'I won't, for sure.' Michael turned to Edward and quietly said, 'Thank you, sir.' He shook hands, slung his small holdall over his shoulder and disappeared through the gate in the massive wire fence.

'How awful,' said Anne. 'He seems a gentle character, and, my God, doesn't Robert look like him? Oh, Dad! How are you going to sort it all out?'

'To tell the truth, I just don't know where to start. I wonder if Bill would be able to do anything for him? Surely a chap should be allowed to make a fresh start.'

Chapter Fourteen

The birthday was a happy occasion. Robert, partly to please Edward and Louise, made a great show of blowing out the ten candles on the cake.

'Happy birthday to you, dear Robert,' sang Edward, Louise and Tim, Robert's best friend at school. After tea they admired the computer in the corner of Robert's bedroom. But later, when Tim had gone home, Robert complained of a sore throat and a headache and thought he would like to go to bed if they did not mind.

Next morning he was not better and by the evening he had a high temperature and was flushed and feeling very ill. The doctor was called and said it was a severe case of flu. He would call again tomorrow.

Next day, he found Robert no better and no worse. On seeing the Robinsons' anxiety, he said he would get his partner to see Robert. 'Between us, we will soon have you better.'

In due course Dr Green examined Robert and suggested that they should run some tests. Two days later the results of the tests were returned. Robert was still running a high temperature and feeling ill, unable to read or bother with his computer.

Edward and Louise were very worried when they were told Robert would have to be moved to hospital. They sensed that his condition was serious.

The doctor said, 'I have to admit, I am puzzled, but surely they will get to the bottom of it. I am sure Robert will soon recover.'

They notified Siobhan, the social worker who visited Robert, and interviewed the ward sister and also the consultant together with Louise and Edward. Robert was not very happy in hospital, but he did not complain. He suddenly looked very thin and small in his hospital bed. His eyes were bright and his cheeks were flushed. He cried a little when Louise was with him and asked her to bring him home.

It was now clear that he was very ill indeed, but it came as a great shock when more tests revealed that Robert had leukaemia. The Robinsons were devastated but gallantly tried to hide their concern from Robert when visiting every day, although they felt no better when it was decided that Robert should be transferred to hospital in Belfast for a course of chemotherapy.

Robert was listless and so ill that he seemed unconcerned about being moved to another hospital. All he wanted was to go home.

Edward explained to him, while Louise held his hand, that he was going to have some treatment that would make him feel very sick but that in the end would make him better, after which he would be able to go home and back to school. This was a very special kind of treatment that he could only have in Belfast. He must be brave, but they would visit him every day.

Robert was in hospital for three months. He was a co-operative little patient, only occasionally breaking down when he felt ill. At these times he would weep quietly and cling to Louise's hand and beg her to take him home and let him stop the treatment. His doctors reported that they were pleased with the way he was responding the treatment and that they were hopeful of the final outcome.

One day the consultant asked to see Louise and Edward before they left for home. He told them there was a further treatment which would benefit Robert if it could be arranged. He explained to them that a bone marrow transplant would almost certainly increase Robert's chances of recovery. The problem was to find a suitable donor whose bone marrow would match and be compatible for Robert. The consultant went on to explain that a near relative usually was the best chance but that he understood that Robert was an orphan. Did he have any close relatives that they knew?

Edward said, 'Actually, we do know where his natural father is. In fact, he is in prison and he is known to us but not to Robert.'

The doctor then asked, 'Do you think the father would be prepared to donate his bone marrow if we can make the necessary arrangements with the Northern Ireland office and the Prison Medical Service?'

If Michael agreed, a sample would be taken; the doctor thought it could be done in the prison hospital. If the sample matched up with Robert's bone marrow, the father would have to be hospitalised and his bone marrow extracted under a general anaesthetic, a fairly serious operation. There would be considerable pain just for a few days after the operation, but of course he would be given medication as required, and it could be very valuable for a child with leukaemia.

The consultants spent further time discussing the best way to go ahead and to make the necessary contacts. Edward was quite sure that Michael would agree to be a donor for Robert.

He said, 'The position is that the father is genuinely concerned about his son.' Edward went on to outline the circumstances which led to his wife and himself taking Robert into their home.

He went on to say, 'We have kept the father well informed about every stage of Robert's development. He knows Robert is ill, but I don't think he realises just how serious his condition is. We did not think that it was fair or necessary to worry him over much at first, but we were considering that we might have to let him know if Robert became any worse. I don't know if he would get compassionate leave or not.'

Then Edward remembered that Michael had said he was due for pre-release leave soon. Surely, under these special circumstances, it should not be impossible to get this leave brought forward rather than trying to get compassionate leave, especially as there would be no mention of Michael having any children on his file.

So, without any further delay, the Chief Medical Officer was approached so that a sample of Michael's bone marrow could be obtained. This did not prove too difficult, but before this could be finally arranged, Michael would have to be told how very ill Robert now was and to have the whole process of the bone marrow transfusion explained to him.

Edward volunteered to see Michael as soon as possible. He thought the best way of getting an extraordinary visit would be by contacting the chaplain and at the same time making a request to see the Governor.

Louise stayed with a friend in Belfast so that she could be with Robert as much as possible. She spent many hours at his bedside. Sometimes he was fairly cheerful but at others, when he felt very sick, especially after his treatments, he just lay with his eyes closed. A very wan child, most of his hair had fallen out and he could hardly raise his head without being overcome with waves of nausea.

Occasionally he would open his eyes and smile at Louise, whispering, 'Lou, don't leave me, will you?'

She would squeeze his hot little hand, smooth his forehead, bend over and kiss him, saying, 'Darling, of course I will never leave you.' Robert then usually dropped into a fretful sleep.

After a time the side effects would gradually lessen and he would be able to get up and join the other children in the day room. On his good days, he would watch television or join in games for short periods after which he would quickly tire.

Louise could see no improvement and was very afraid he was going to slip away from them, although his doctors said he was holding his own against the dread disease and if he could get the transplant he would have a very good chance of making a full recovery. It was important that this was not delayed for too long.

Louise tried never to let Robert know how anxious they were. The memory of James, that other little boy that they had loved and lost, was now constantly with her. 'Please, God,' she prayed, 'don't let Robert die. Please let the transplant take place and be successful.'

Within three days Edward gratefully got permission to have a special interview with Michael. He was faced with the task of telling him how very ill Robert was. He felt guilty that they had not kept him better informed, but even when they were weighed down with anxiety there had seemed no point in telling Michael.

Face to face, Edward told him very carefully, 'Robert has a serious illness, leukaemia. He is in a very critical condition. Now there is a chance he will make a complete recovery if he were to have a transplant of healthy bone marrow. The disease he is suffering from causes his bone marrow to fail and this is a life-threatening condition. An infusion of bone marrow has to match from donor to recipient – do you follow me? To accomplish this, the donor usually has to be a close relative, that much we do know. Would you do this for Robert? It means an operation, perhaps a few days with some pain, but I am told that within a week or so your system will replace any loss quite naturally and you should suffer no ill effects and Robert will get well again. Will you undergo the tests to see if you and Robert are compatible?'

Michael was very shocked at the news about Robert, but with no hesitation he immediately said, 'Of course I will do this and anything, but anything, to help Robert. After all, he is my son.'

'Good! Then we will go ahead and request that you are given the necessary leave. I must go now because there are many arrangements to be made. Try not to worry too much about Robert. Please God and thanks to your generosity, Robert will pull through.'

But Michael did worry. What if he did not get leave or if he did not turn out to be a suitable donor? Was that what Edward said he would be? Oh, he hoped Robert would get well again. He did feel frightened about having an operation. He had never been in hospital, except one night in the prison hospital after he had been badly beaten up shortly after he had been transferred to Magilligan. That had not been too bad.

As Edward was about to leave he got a message that the Governor would like to see him. The Governor told Edward that he had received word from the Chief Medical Prison Officer that Prisoner Michael Duffy 1671 might be going to act as a donor for a ten-year-old boy. Edward explained that Michael Duffy was the boy's natural father, and that he was the foster parent. It was a very unusual chain of events.

The Governor, a family man himself with two boys of his own, recognised Edward's distress and promised to do anything to facilitate the smooth progress of the affair. He admitted he had been suspicious of the whole story because he said that prisoners are not above fabricating any story to suit their own ends.

'I will, in this case, recommend that Northern Ireland Office allow leave whenever the hospital ask for it. Mind you, I can only make a recommendation. The Parole Board are very much their own masters. However,' he continued, in this case it should work out. I see from Duffy's file he does not appear to have been a difficult prisoner. Does the boy know about his father? Does he know where he is?'

Edward sighed, 'The boy is only ten years old and rightly or wrongly we have not as yet told him that his father is alive. He thinks he is dead. This has been a constant worry. Now all we can think about is will he get better. If he does, and please God he will, in all fairness to Michael we will have to tell him. As a child, Robert has always been so easy, such a good, sunny-natured character. We feared, my wife and I, to distress him when he was still young. Perhaps we were wrong. I just don't know. We will meet this when Robert is better.'

The Governor agreed it was an extraordinary problem. As he shook hands with Edward, he said, 'I really wish the little boy well, and also Duffy.'

Chapter Fifteen

Michael was admitted to the prison hospital where a visiting doctor, a technician, accompanied by the Prison Medical Officer, collected a sample from Michael under local anaesthetic. They also made a number of tests and had some X-rays taken. Michael was in a state of agitation, with very mixed feelings; first and foremost he was intensely worried because Robert was so ill and also he was frightened at the thought of having an operation. This was something quite outside his experience, but he was steadfast in his determination to go ahead with it, should his bone marrow match Robert's. He now felt confident that it would.

The proceedings were carefully explained to him. They also told him that in the meanwhile they would keep him in the prison hospital until the results of the tests came through. This would only be for a very few days, perhaps only two. There was a degree of urgency. Robert should not have to wait too long for his transplant. The sooner the better it would be for him; he was a very sick child.

It was fortunate that Michael was due to get parole. This would speed things up. They assured Michael that they were quite hopeful; more than that they could not say.

The days of waiting for the results were full of anguish. Michael was very restless. He could not relax because he just did not know what was going to happen to Robert or to himself. He was glad to help the hospital orderlies with the serving of meals and with the cleaning of the hospital unit, and he prayed as he had never prayed before.

Michael thought, If there is a God, surely He will not let him die. At other times he thought this was God's way of letting him do something for his son, a chance to make up for deserting him and for the shame which his prison background would bring to Robert.

Word came through that his application for parole had been granted, also that all the tests were satisfactory and he was to report to the Royal Victoria Hospital on the following day, for which a pass would be made out for him. Later, there was a message that a Mr Robinson would be waiting for him outside the main gate at nine thirty.

Michael felt a rush of gratitude towards Edward, because he had been worrying about making his way to Belfast on his own. He had only been outside the prison once in almost eight years, which was when he had been on Christmas parole. He recalled how disorientated he had been then and how he had spent much of the time in the hostel watching television, except when he had accepted the invitation to spend the day with the Robinsons, a memory he treasured.

The meeting with Robert had been a bittersweet experience, a strange kind of happiness. He had marvelled that the lovely child with a quick smile and a beautiful speaking voice could really be his son. He had kept his promise and had not made himself known to Robert, remembering that Edward had been concerned about this, worrying in case Michael would be unable to keep his word. In the event, it had been a happy occasion. Robert had accepted that Louise was always a kind person and that she was entertaining a man from prison who had nowhere to go for his Christmas.

All these thoughts kept going through Michael's mind. At first Robert had been merely polite and rather shy, but as the day wore on he had thawed and had chatted about television and football. He even promised to write to Michael, saying they could be penfriends.

This had not happened and now Robert might be dying. 'Oh God, let him live. Let me die if anyone has to die.'

Edward, as arranged, was at the prison gates and he drove Michael to Belfast. Both men were consumed with anxiety and spoke little during the drive to the hospital.

'Will I be able to see Robert?' asked Michael.

Edward replied, 'Robert is now kept in strict isolation, but I think you will be allowed to see him for a short while. Some days he is quite bright and on other days he is feeling very sick and can hardly raise his head from the pillow.'

Michael was totally overwhelmed when they arrived at the hospital. It was vast and there were so many people all moving in different directions. He could not tell who they all were, but he assumed they were doctors, nurses and patients. He had no idea how many people were involved in the day-to-day running of a hospital.

Edward, who knew his way around, shepherded him to the reception and admissions area saying, 'I will leave you here, Michael, and I will see you later.'

When Michael gave his name to a pleasant, middle-aged lady, she said, 'Oh yes, Michael. We are expecting you. Please, will you just give me these details and then I will get somebody to take you up to your ward.'

On arriving at the ward landing, a pretty young nurse was waiting for him. 'I am Judith and I will be your nurse while you are here. Please come with me. I will show you your room, then I must ask you some details for the record.'

The side ward, which was to be Michael's room, was very small and not unlike the cell that he had occupied for years at Magilligan, the only difference being that Michael could see that there were no bars on the window and no locks on the door.

Michael answered the questions as best he could. Some, regarding family and occupation, he found embarrassing to give satisfactory answers. Judith made it easy for him, saying, 'It is all right. I do know about you and all the staff here admire what you are doing for the little boy Robert. Now, you must go to bed.'

Michael was grateful to her but he felt quite strange going to bed when he felt quite well. However, he did not have too much time to worry about this because a succession of people kept coming into his room: a white-coated technician to take some blood from his arm, a social worker to ask more questions, a young doctor to take his medical history. These were followed by a priest who said he was the hospital chaplain.

'Would you like to go to confession?' he asked.

Michael declined, saying, 'Thank you, but really I don't feel the need just now.'

The priest accepted his decision and said, 'I will pray for you and for your intentions and for the successful outcome of your operations and little Robert's recovery.'

This pleased Michael and he wondered if he had been churlish in refusing to make a confession. He remembered priests always wanted him to make a confession.

Following the priest a group came and almost filled the room: a portly, grey-haired, white-coated and distinguished-looking man introduced himself as Michael's surgeon and then introduced his assistants and the Sister.

'I will operate on you the day after tomorrow. Before then there will be some more tests for you and some X-rays.' Then he said to the assistant, 'You had better arrange for him to go to physiotherapy tomorrow.'

Turning to Michael again, the surgeon said, 'I am hopeful that as a result of this operation you are about to have, Robert will recover. I hope that you will not be too uncomfortable, but if you are, it will only be for a short time, and Sister here and her team will look after you very well, and yes, you can see Robert. Under the circumstances we cannot deny you that.'

Not long after the surgeon and his entourage had left, Edward came in to see Michael. 'This is a brave thing you are doing.' Hesitatingly, he added, 'Michael, we don't know if Robert is well enough to learn that you are his father. We feel it is right that he should know as soon as he is well. Just now he is very ill and he is only ten. We will tell him you are his donor and that you are helping him to get well. When he is older he will always be grateful to you. I understand you will be seeing him shortly. You may be shocked when you see him because his hair has fallen out and he looks very poorly.'

Michael was indeed shocked when he saw Robert a little later. He seemed such a pathetic little figure with his completely bald head, large eyes with dark shadows in a pale face, so small in his hospital bed – hardly recognisable as the lively boy of the previous Christmas.

Michael went to his bedside and said, very quietly, 'Robert, do you remember me? I was to be your pen friend.'

Robert smiled and only then did Michael get a glimpse of the former Robert.

'Yes, I remember you. I was the only boy who had a prisoner for a penfriend.'

Michael inwardly burned with shame. Louise, who was sitting by the other side of Robert's bed, then came to his rescue, saying, 'Soon Michael will be leaving prison and making a fresh start, but now he has come to donate some of his bone marrow to you because this will make you better. Doctors have discovered a cure which can be made by transfusing bone marrow from a well person to a sick boy or girl like you. Rather like a blood transfusion, except this is done while you are asleep.'

Robert said politely, 'Thank you, Michael. I do know about transplants. One of the doctors told me about them.'

Michael was too overcome to know what to say, so just said, 'I will see you later and I hope you will be feeling better.'

When Michael was alone in his room he thought about Robert. He realised that in all his life he had never loved anybody as he loved his son. He did not understand why, but he just knew that Robert was the most important thing in his life. It was strange that this love was so strong because he had only seen Robert twice, but then he had loved him ever since Jim had told him that Elsie had a son. Perhaps it was because no one had ever belonged to him.

He recalled Joe, the St Vincent de Paul visitor, back in Crumlin Road. He did feel deeply about him and he had grieved when Joe had died, but that was different. He knew he admired Edward and Louise and liked them very much, especially Louise, but again that was different. Gratitude, he supposed.

'Oh God! I hope Robert will get better. He did look so frail and so ill.' When all this was over he hoped that it would not be too long. This was like a bad dream, but it was no dream. It was very much for real, otherwise Robert would not be lying in this hospital nor would he be here about to donate bone marrow to his son. When all this was behind them and Robert well again, he wondered if Edward and Louise would allow him to tell Robert that he was his father. It would be wonderful just to make himself known. He would explain to Robert that it would be best for him to stay with Edward and Louise, whom he loved and who loved him, because he could never do for him what they were doing for him by accepting him as part of their family, but just for him to know he had a father who also loved him.

He also wondered about donating his bone marrow to Robert. He knew little about medical matters. He was pleased that he was doing this. It appeared that no one else could do this, so he was giving a gift to Robert. A gift of life-giving properties to save life. He felt good about it.

Chapter Sixteen

Michael did not see Robert for several days because he was preparing for his operation the following evening. A young doctor explained to him that the bone marrow would be extracted from his sternum, or breast bone. He would not feel a thing because he would be asleep, and although it might be painful after the operation for a time, not to worry – he would soon be as right as rain and it was all in a good cause.

Judith was most understanding. She said, 'I will look after you. I am sure you must be feeling apprehensive – so many tests and different people coming and going. As I said, I am your nurse and I will be with you most of the time until you are recovered completely – I hope that won't take too long. Now, I must shave your chest and then paint on this orange antiseptic lotion so that you are ready for the surgeon tomorrow morning.'

Edward looked in that evening and wished him well. That night Michael slept a sound, deep, dreamless sleep, and early in the morning he was given an injection which left him drowsy. He knew little more until he awoke, conscious of a startlingly severe pain in his chest, which seemed to tear him apart. He could not remember where he was. The room was spinning round. All he was aware of was the pain, like a red-hot poker in his chest.

Somebody was saying, 'It is over now, Michael. You have done very well.'

Next morning the pain was still there but it was less intense and he remembered that he was in hospital. Then he thought about Robert. He must find out how he was, but he was surprised to find he could not get out of bed. He would have to ask somebody, a nurse or a doctor.

'How are you today?' asked a nurse.

Michael thought it was Judith, but he still felt muzzy and was not quite sure. 'I am fine now. Tell me, how is Robert?'

'Robert is doing well. The doctors are very pleased with the way he is progressing. He may be going to have his first transfusion today; I am not quite sure.'

This was good news for Michael, and on the following day he was able to get up and walk very stiffly along the corridor to Sister's office to ask if he could see Robert.

'Just for a few minutes, then.'

When he went into Robert's little room, the boy was just waking. He did not recognise Michael, but he smiled because he was naturally friendly, even when sick, a good-natured and well-mannered boy and also because he felt that somehow it was expected of him.

Later that day, Edward and Louise came to see Michael, who was feeling a great deal better. They assured him that the doctors were very pleased with the result of his operation and that they were optimistic that Robert would greatly benefit. They also said that Michael's own system would shortly reconstitute and replace the bone marrow that had been taken from him. Edward emphasised that this operation had been a life-saving act on Michael's part.

Then he went on to say, 'Everybody is full of admiration for you. Doctors, nurses and the other patients are so happy that Robert's chances of recovery are now so much greater.' Edward paused, and went on to say, 'I am making enquiries on your behalf. I hope to come up with something.'

Michael felt a glow of happiness. His pain was much less and he had the prospect of only a few more months in prison, but above all, he felt he had proved himself. He had been of real use to Robert. He had been on hand when he was needed. Every day he felt better, almost quite well again. He was allowed to wander about the ward to chat with the other patients. No one ever mentioned that he was a prisoner out on special leave; he was not sure if they knew or not. He was told he would have to remain in hospital for another ten days or even a little longer, until his bone marrow count was back to normal.

The days passed pleasantly. He used to drop into Robert's room and spend a few minutes with him, but most of the time Robert was still feeling ill and not inclined to talk much.

Louise spent most of every day with Robert and he sensed that she was very anxious, even though the doctors said he was stable and they must be patient.

Michael asked if it would be possible for him to send out for some drawing paper and pencils so that he could pass the time sketching. An orderly brought these in for him and he spent many hours of the long days drawing. The other patients were pleased and amused with the rough sketches he did for them. He took great pains with one of Judith, who he did not see so much of as he was now up and about.

Michael made himself useful helping with meals and with washing up in the ward kitchen. He appeared to be making a complete recovery and he was considering how he would feel when he was discharged and back in Magilligan.

On the tenth day after his operation as he awoke Michael very suddenly became agitated and confused, complaining of a very severe pain in his chest and sweating profusely. Judith, who had just come on duty, saw he was deathly pale. She immediately went to call the house physician. Before he arrived, Michael had collapsed and although the resuscitation team was there within minutes and worked valiantly to revive him, much to their great dismay he was dead. The chaplain anointed him, although he could not be sure he was still alive. It was said that Michael had suffered a pulmonary embolism. Nothing could have been done to save him.

The entire ward, staff and patients, who knew him were shocked and saddened, because he was well-liked by everybody who had come across him and he was about to be discharged.

Edward, Louise and Anne were the only mourners at Michael Duffy's funeral. After requiem mass, as they followed the coffin from the church to the cemetery, they were joined by a tall, middle-aged man they had not noticed before. He was carrying a large wreath.

As they made their way to the graveside, this man came up to Edward and said, 'You will not know me. My name is Tom McFadden. I was Michael Duffy's chief officer at Magilligan. He was a quiet young man who never gave us any trouble. When we heard what had happened, the other lads asked me to come today and they sent this wreath, all chipping in with something from their earnings, which are pretty small. There is some good in most of them. They were genuinely sorry to hear Michael had died. They are also concerned about the boy.'

Edward said, 'I am afraid Robert is not out of the woods yet by any means, but we hope he will pull through. Thank you for coming today. We do appreciate the wreath from the men in prison – as you rightly say, there is some good in most people. We feel very sad about Michael. He was coming to the end of his sentence and he was about to make a fresh start.'

When the priest's few prayers were said and the final blessing given, the coffin was lowered into the grave.

Three wreaths were laid on the newly filled-in grave, one from the Robinson family, another from Robert and the very large one from the prisoners at Magilligan. They shook hands with the priest and made their way towards their cars.

Tom McFadden went ahead and took a large parcel from the boot of his car and handed it to Edward, saying, 'The staff and I thought you would like to have these. They are some of Michael's paintings. He was quite an artist, you know.'

Again, Edward thanked him for coming and for the portfolio. Apparently, Michael had no other possessions. There might be a small sum of money which he had saved; this would be forwarded to them in due course. Edward put the portfolio in the car and they drove back to the hospital to see Robert.

They found, to their dismay, that Robert had been moved to intensive care. The sister assured them that this was merely a precaution, as he was having a slight reaction to the transfusion and there he could be continually observed until he was stable again.

Robert was asleep when they got to intensive care. The Sister here again assured them there was nothing to be alarmed about.

She said, 'There are no signs that he is rejecting the transplant; merely a slight reaction.'

When Robert awoke, he clutched Louise's hand. Crying a little, he said, 'Oh Lou, where have you been? I feel so sick and my head hurts and I am either too hot or awfully cold. I don't like this ward. When will I be able to go back to my room?'

Louise bent over and kissed him. 'You won't be here for very long, just until you feel a bit better. I am sorry I was not here this morning. I had to go out for a short while. From now on, one of us will stay with you. Try to sleep now.'

Seeing Robert lying there, so quiet and looking so frail, Louise wondered if this small, pitiful figure could ever regain his health and grow strong to become the Robert they had taken into their family and grown to love. Then her thoughts turned to Michael – only a few days ago he had looked so well and now death had snatched him away when he had done a noble thing.

Tears of sorrow and exhaustion filled her eyes. She must not let Robert see her like this. The next few days passed very slowly and Robert slept fitfully most of the time. He appeared to be hovering between life and death. Louise was filled with despair.

The doctors and nurses were kind and gentle with her and cheerful and efficient as they tended to Robert. On the fourth day, not long after dawn, as Louise took up her vigil at Robert's bedside, relieving Edward who had been there all night, suddenly Robert opened his eyes wide and smiled.

'Hello, Lou. Hello, Da. Do you know, I am starving? Can I have something to eat, please?'

'Of course! What would you like? I will ask the nurse. She will be so pleased.'

Robert had turned the corner and he was almost immediately well again. He was now allowed back to his room on the other landing. The doctors explained that, just as they had hoped, Robert's system was now accepting the transplant and although he had a long way to go before he would be fully recovered, his future was now looking extremely bright.

Chapter Seventeen

Robert did eventually make an excellent recovery. He was able to go home having been in hospital for just over six months. Doctors warned Louise that they could expect Robert to be difficult and temperamental. He was very quiet, but not in the least difficult, clearly happy to be home and especially pleased to be reunited with Folly. He talked with enthusiasm about going back to school now that his hair was beginning to grow again.

One day he said to Louise, 'Who was Michael? A nurse told me when people have a transplant of bone marrow like I did, the bone marrow usually has to come from a close relative, or it does not work. Was Michael my brother? Was he the same Michael who came to spend Christmas with us and who painted that picture of Folly for me? He was nice. Nurse told me he was let out of prison to donate his bone marrow to me and he died. That was dreadful.'

Louise was taken back by this, although she always knew Robert would one day ask about Michael. Quietly she said, 'It was indeed very sad about Michael and that he died. I think I will ask Da to help me explain. It is a very long story and sad.'

Louise went to find Edward and said, 'Robert is asking about Michael. We will have to tell him, Edward. He has to know sometime and perhaps now is the right time.'

'Robert,' said Edward, 'Michael was not your brother – he was your father and yes, he was in prison. Your mother and he were not legally married and Michael did not know about you until after he was in prison. Incidentally, he was extremely foolish and allowed himself to be sucked into the IRA. He handled some explosive material for them and was caught red-handed, a very serious offence for which he received ten years' imprisonment. When he learnt you were in a welfare children's home he contacted Louise and myself and asked us to visit him in prison. He had once worked for us. When we saw him he told us that he had a son and asked us to visit you. I think now that from the very first he hoped we would become your foster parents or adopt you. I think in the one week that he worked in this house and garden he sensed Lou had a very kind heart. Of course he was right. He himself had been an orphan. He knew all about growing up in a children's home where there was nobody especially to care about him, and he did not want this to happen to you. The rest you know.'

'How lucky we were to have you, to care for and to love,' said Louise.

'Now, you must not think too badly about Michael,' continued Edward. 'He did make a very bad mistake but he really did love you and in the end he saved your life and it cost him his own life.'

'Why did he die?' asked Robert.

'Well, as I understand, it was a very outside chance. He had a complication called a pulmonary embolism which in his case was fatal. There is always some degree of risk, usually very small, with any operation.'

'Did you and Lou like Michael?'

'Well, we did not really know him very well, but he was thoughtful and considerate when he assisted Lou when she fell in the road. He stopped, helped her to her feet and helped her home. That was how he came to work for us. That act of kindness changed the course of history, at least as far as you are concerned.'

Edward and Louise watched and waited anxiously to see how Robert would react to learning about his father.

'I think it was a brilliant idea of Michael's to ask you and Da to look after me when he could not himself. If he had not died, what would have happened when he came out of prison?'

'Well, Robert, that is something we will never know. I hope we would have found a satisfactory solution.'

'I think it was a brilliant idea, and I also think Michael was a super person, even if he was in prison, because he came and was there when I really needed him. I will always know that he saved my life. He painted Folly here for me.'

Robert bent over and hugged the large dog, hiding his face in the thick, black coat to hide tears that were rolling down his face. Nothing more was said about Michael but quite often all three of the family would think about him with thoughts they would have found difficult to put into words.

Robert's recovery seemed to be complete. At three-monthly intervals and then six-monthly check-ups the doctors reported that they were more than pleased with his progress. He went back to school, soon made up for lost time and kept up well with his class. He successfully passed into St Mura's College.

His only concern was that he was not growing very fast. He appeared to be quite slight compared with the other boys of his age. His doctor assured him that in time he would grow, if not to six foot, to a reasonable height and that he must not be too concerned about his lack of stature. He must remember that he had suffered a serious illness, which had set him back more than a little. He also recommended that Robert should not play rugger or any competitive games for at least another year and maybe not even then. He could exercise but in moderation. He went on to suggest that Edward should interest him in fishing.

Robert accepted these limitations with good grace. So that he would not appear stand-offish to the boys, he would stand on the sidelines on Saturdays and watch rugger practice; he watched at home matches and cheered on the school most enthusiastically.

Edward took him fishing once or twice, but Robert politely told him he did not think he would ever make an angler. Louise suggested he took up birdwatching. Robert was doubtful about this, feeling that perhaps it was not a very manly hobby.

Finally the school started a photographic club. Robert asked Edward if he would lend him some money to augment his savings so that he could buy a camera. Edward agreed and this project proved to be a great success; before long Robert's bedroom walls were adorned with photos, first of Folly and later of Louise and Edward together and singly, followed by boys at school in and out of class.

Chapter Eighteen

As time went by, Robert's illness was almost forgotten. His school work, his friends and his photography fully occupied his days. Edward and Louise at first worried that something about Michael might leak out and cause Robert embarrassment and pain. They knew Robert treasured his memory of Michael as a sort of hero because he had saved his life and that he altogether discounted the fact that he had been in prison. Robert's headmaster knew Robert's history. He assured the Robinsons that this information would be strictly confidential and that no one need ever know anything which would cause unnecessary pain to Robert.

Anne was spending a long weekend with her parents and she was delighted to find Robert well. She had become most attached to him, ever since he had come to live with the family. She had come over from London when he was ill and had suffered almost as much as Louise and Edward had done throughout the time Robert had the transplants and when Michael had died. Now she admired Robert's photographs and gave him a handsome cheque towards his expenses, as she put it. He was able to repay Edward's loan and still have some over to buy a tripod and other equipment.

After Robert was in bed, Anne asked Edward, 'Have you ever looked at Michael's portfolio? Could I see what his work was like?'

Edward replied, 'I only glanced at it. We did not have the heart to do anything about it. Maybe you are right – we should have a look through it now.'

The pictures were all neatly labelled in a beautiful script. The earlier work was in a traditional style: studies of farmyards and some very good sketches of flowers and birds, also a number of interiors, the style becoming bolder and the colours brighter. There was what was obviously a study of his cell and, further on, among other sketches and studies, there was a picture which must have been from memory. It was an impression of the sitting room they were in now. Almost every detail was right.

'Just look at that,' said Anne. 'There can be no mistaking where that is. How amazing.'

Then Anne turned up a startling canvas. A man sitting in what appeared to be a prison cell. He was looking down and wringing his hands which were covered in blood, spilling onto the floor. On his lap was an object which might have been a grenade or bomb. The most striking aspect was that the man had a baby's head and face. The face was that of a very young child who was crying. The title of this was 'Never Let It Happen.'

There were several versions of this, all similar and all quite startling and grotesque.

'These are nightmarish things,' said Anne. 'Michael must have been in anguish when he did these, but you must realise these are very good. Of that I am quite sure. I wonder if we could do anything with them.'

After a pause she said, 'If you would let me, I will take them to London and show them to some people I know who could advise about their possible value. I personally think they are both interesting and valuable.'

Louise thought and then said, 'I wonder if we sold them if we should give the money or at least some of the money to charity. Leukaemia research would be appropriate, don't you think?'

'Well, who knows. I might be quite wrong,' said Anne. 'Also, Robert is sure to want to keep some.'

Anne was not mistaken. The pictures were considered to be extremely interesting. She took the portfolio back to London with her. It did not take her long before she found a friend who had the right contacts in the art world. Somewhat to her surprise, and against her wildest expectations, Michael's work attracted immediate interest. Within six months of her introducing herself as Michael's agent and mentor, a retrospective exhibition was arranged for a small but fashionable art gallery in Cork Street, off Bond Street.

Anne decided to announce that twenty-five per cent of any sales made would be given to leukaemia research. As a friend of the late Michael Duffy this would be his wish. If asked, she planned to say the remainder would be invested for the education of his twelve-year-old son. She also contacted a doctor, who she knew had specialised in the care and treatment of leukaemia patients, to open the exhibition.

The critics gave a most favourable press release. Some even went as far as to compare some of the collection with Van Gogh and Edvard Munch. But somehow, details of Michael's background leaked out, that he had been a convicted terrorist and that he had produced all of the collection to be shown while in prison in Northern Ireland. It was also revealed that his young son had suffered from leukaemia, that he had donated his bone marrow and that this most certainly saved the boy's life even though he had died in so doing. This added an enormous emotional and human dimension.

The small gallery was packed on the opening day and on the following days. Anne spent as much time there as she could and she was almost overwhelmed with questions about Michael and also about Robert. These she found difficult to answer because she knew her parents would not want Robert drawn into the limelight. She wondered what bringing up the whole sad story that was Michael's would do to Robert. She began to be doubtful now about the wisdom of having a public exhibition. The very last thing she wanted was that Robert would be caused any distress or indeed her parents either.

Anne reproached herself: 'What have I done? Human pain and tragedy are the raw material of news. Nobody cares if individuals suffer. All this may destroy Robert and poor unloved Michael. The press will not now let him rest in peace.'

Every day the press flaunted the Michael Duffy story. 'Terrorist Turned Artist' and 'Pictures From Prison' were some of the headlines in the tabloids. What distressed Anne was that there was scant mention that Michael had donated his bone marrow to his son, that the transplant almost certainly saved Robert's life and that it had cost Michael his life.

Anne felt a little happier when she was approached by a man who wanted to produce a book of reproductions of Michael's art which would be sold and the proceeds given to leukaemia research.

On the final day of the exhibition, when all pictures offered sale were sold for figures well beyond anything Anne had expected, the Robinsons had requested that some, including the interior of their drawing room and a small self-portrait and a few others which they particularly liked, should be exhibited but withheld from the sale.

A pleasant, grey-haired lady approached Anne and introduced herself saying, 'You will not know me, but I was Michael Duffy's art teacher in Magilligan. I heard Michael had died but I did not know the circumstances surrounding his death. In fact, I really know very little about his life, but he was a quiet young man, modest about his work. I soon realised after he joined my classes that he had talent and I am happy and even a little proud to think that I, in some way, encouraged and brought out this talent. I never knew what became of his paintings. It would have been a tragedy if his work had never been discovered. As it is, it is very sad that he died. He can't have been very old. What did he die of? Was it leukaemia?'

Anne explained, 'It was not Michael but Robert, his son, who had leukaemia. Sadly and quite unexpectedly Michael died. You know, he donated his bone marrow to the little boy and this is thought to have saved his life. Following the operation to extract the bone marrow, Michael died. It was awful because it was ten days after and we all thought he was recovering. The only good thing about the whole sad story is that Robert did recover and is now quite well. He was very ill but the doctors hoped all along that the transplant would be successful and they had told Michael that they were optimistic about Robert's future. So poor Michael did at least know this before he died. His death was sudden and unexpected – a pulmonary embolism, we were told.'

Mary Moore and Anne left the gallery together. 'Would you join me for dinner? I would like to know a little more about Michael Duffy and his son.'

Anne was glad to unfold the story to this soft-spoken woman because she was having misgivings about the effect the publicity might have on Robert. She kept wondering, 'Was the exhibition a mistake?'

Mary was older and experienced enough to know the publicity would soon die away. She reassured Anne, saying, 'I hope I am right, but I know the pictures are very good and it is right that they should be recognised for their true value. I understand some money will be donated to medical research. This is important and can always be emphasised to Robert. If he holds onto these aspects of it, plus the fact that Michael virtually saved his life, I do not think that the fact that he was in prison should trouble Robert too much.'

Anne need not have agonised about the effect the publicity would have on Robert because when the story reached the north-west of Ireland during the month of August, during the long summer holiday, a time of unusual quietness in Londonderry, reporters found that the Robinsons were away from home.

After several unsuccessful attempts to locate them they gave up and followed another story. Mary Moore was proved right. Robert was spared all the publicity that Anne had worried about.

Edward, Louise and Robert were staying in London with Anne. They had interrupted their journey to holiday in France to keep an important engagement. Louise, with Edward and Robert and Anne at her side, received a bouquet of flowers as she handed over a cheque for £1000 to the chairman of the Leukaemia Research Fund.

As they drove out to the airport to start their holiday, Edward said, 'I think Michael has really atoned for his sins...'

Part Two
Full Circle

Chapter Nineteen

In 1992 Robert was twenty-one and in that summer he
graduated with an honours degree from Cambridge.

When he first went up, he had elected to read English
and he greatly enjoyed this. He was a keen student, attending his lectures without fail. He read widely and deeply,
producing excellent essays for his tutors. Cambridge was
sheer luxury for him. He got on well with his fellow
undergraduates, even though he took no part in sporting
activities. It was known that he came from a distant part of
Northern Ireland. Occasionally he was asked about the
political situation there. He would answer as best he could,
but he never made any personal revelations, nor was he
asked for any.

Sometimes he would watch the occasional rugger match
or, in summer, cricket, and he liked to play chess when he
could find somebody to play with, but in the main he spent
his free time alone, at first exploring the colleges and
soaking up the atmosphere. Later he discovered the
Fitzwilliam Museum and he spent many hours there. At
other times he attended Evensong in the Chapel of King's
College. It came as no surprise to those who knew him
when he changed his course and decided to study
Theology.

Robert lived modestly while at college and during the
long vacation he travelled on the continent, visiting Paris,
Florence and Rome one year and Berlin and Austria and
Switzerland another. For shorter breaks he returned to

Ireland to be with Louise and Edward, sometimes stopping off on the way to stay with Anne.

While in London they would take in a concert or a play and he visited the National Galleries and the Tate Gallery. On one occasion Anne took him to a newly opened Gallery of Contemporary Art where there were two pictures by Michael Duffy.

While they were there, Robert asked, 'Do you think I should have changed my name and taken my father's name?'

'No,' answered Anne. 'We did wonder about that some years ago, and being worldly-wise, we decided against this. Having his name might have done you a disservice on some occasions. What is in a name that could make any difference to Michael? Do well at Cambridge. He would have liked that and that is more important.'

Later that evening Robert asked Anne, 'Could you check and see if I was ever baptised? I need to know.'

'I will check, of course, but I am quite sure the Children's Department will have looked into this. Such details are important, especially in Ireland... why, Robert? Are you thinking of getting married?'

She wondered privately if perhaps he might have homosexual inclinations.

He reddened and said, 'I know what you are thinking, Anne. It is not that I don't like girls, because I do, especially pretty girls, but last time I was having a check-up in Belfast the doctor told me it was most unlikely that I ever could have children, which is the result of the chemotherapy treatment that I had when I was ill.'

'I see, but you should not let that worry you much. Kids are a mixed blessing. Anyhow, you could always adopt. There will always be a boy or girl out there. History has a way of repeating itself.'

Anne said no more, but she studied Robert carefully. He apparently had made a full recovery, but his illness had left its mark on him physically and, she suspected, spiritually. He was small, slight of stature, some might say stunted. Except when he was smiling, which he did very often, there was a strained look about his pale face. He looked frail and delicate. However, his spirit was indomitable. He was always cheerful and even fun loving in his own quiet way.

Anne and Louise were always anxious about his health, but Edward took a different view and would say, 'Robert is tough and he is a survivor, otherwise he would never have overcome the leukaemia and other stressful things in his not very long life. Don't worry.'

As Robert was leaving, he said, 'Anne, I think I am going into the Church – that is if I am accepted. They may not like my background, at least some of it.'

'Of course they will accept you, and they should be jolly glad to get somebody as nice as you. Have you told the parents yet?'

'Well, no. I will tell them when I get home. Do you think they would come over for my graduation next summer? I would really like them to come, if you think it would not be too much for them.'

'I think it is a marvellous idea. I could drive them to Cambridge from London and they could stay for a few days. It would be lovely for them.'

Edward and Louise enjoyed the graduation ceremony, and after it was over they posed for Anne to take photographs on the Senate House lawn. During tea in College they were introduced to the Dean and shook hands with Robert's tutors.

At a celebratory dinner later that evening, Robert looked at the three people he loved: Louise and Edward, so dear to him for as long as he could remember, and Anne, so full of fun but also so down-to-earth and with whom he had a true rapport.

He became very serious. 'I am so pleased you are here today. I know I have been privileged to have spent three years here and I did want you to share this particular day with me. My time here has gone so quickly and I have enjoyed it. Of course, I have been fortunate, as fortunate as my father was unfortunate in life. I owe so much to you, Lou and Edward, and to you, Anne. I also owe a debt to my father, not only that I have enjoyed a generous allowance from the trust you arranged for me from the sale of his paintings and drawings. Something must have inspired him when he asked you to befriend me and to be so wise. It has all turned out so well for me, just as he hoped it would. It is difficult to find the right words to say how much I appreciate all you have done for me and how much I love you all. I now feel I must try to put something back when I start out in the real world. I think I did mention to you before that I was considering going into the Church and now I know this is what I intend to do with my life. I hope you will approve.'

'Well, of course we do, and thank you for those kind words. We are proud of you, Robert,' said Edward.

Anne laughed, and smiling, said, 'Let us now drink to Robert's future and wish him every happiness.'

Anne returned to London by train, leaving her car for Robert to take Edward and Louise out and about and to show them a little of East Anglia.

Robert picked them up at their hotel the next morning. 'Good morning,' said Robert. 'First I would like to show you round my own college, Peterhouse, which I believe is the oldest of all the colleges, founded in 1284. Then we can have coffee in my room which I have not yet vacated. Then I would like you just to look at Caius, St Johns and Trinity and before we finish the day you must see King's College Chapel with the wonderful stained-glass windows.'

When they got back to their hotel Louise said, 'Oh Robert, Cambridge is such a beautiful place. The colleges are lovely, not only because of their architectural features but also their well-kept lawns and terraces with all those bright flowers. Cambridge certainly is a place apart.'

Edward wryly said, 'I would like to have been a young man poling a punt, sporting a straw boater with Louise, as pretty as a picture, under a parasol. Robert, did you ever take a young lady undergraduate on the river?'

Robert laughed and said, 'I am afraid I never did. It was not quite my scene.'

'That is indeed a pity.'

The weather kept fine and they were memorable days for all of them. Edward and Louise were happy about Robert's future plans to go into the Church and although neither were particularly religious, they thought it was an apt choice for Robert, who had a serious side to his character.

On the day before Anne was to collect them to bring them to the airport, the trio lunched at the Angel Inn, Bury St Edmunds. They strolled in the old Abbey gardens and then Robert drove towards the villages of the Bumpsteads. Their road took them past Highpoint Prison. Louise shuddered, recalling another prison where they had first met Robert's father so long ago. Edward also wished they had come another way so that they were not reminded of Magilligan and bittersweet memories.

Robert, ever sensitive to their feelings, knew they were thinking of his father, whom he could only vaguely remember, but he was aware of his sad history and wished it could have ended differently. Michael's ghost was with all three of them for a short while and then faded away. They continued their drive through Constable country to the delightful village of Clare and on to the old wool town of Lavenham where they had a cream tea.

Louise was enchanted with the picturesque hamlets they passed through, with their imposing churches and contrasting small, thatched, colour-washed houses and everywhere masses of roses and summer flowers climbing over every available space in a riot of colour.

Louise said, 'Thank you, Robert. It all has been so lovely. These few days I will cherish.'

'And I second that.'

The Robinsons returned to Ireland; Robert remained in Cambridge to wind up his affairs in College and then to travel north to attend a Bishops Selection Conference concerning his application for a place in a seminary in the Diocese of York, where he expected to spend two more years in study and worship, developing and testing his vocation, undergoing practical, professional and pastoral training with placements in schools, hospitals and parishes, prior to being ordained in the Anglican Church.

That completed, he travelled to Ireland. Throughout the long and in-depth interviews none of the interviewers made any comment on the fact that his father had been in prison.

Chapter Twenty

In 1999 Robert was a full-time chaplain in a huge new prison not far from the city centre of Manchester which had replaced the old prison of Strangeways. He had free access to all parts of the prison. He had his own set of keys. There were five hundred inmates and Robert usually knew most by name. He knew their backgrounds and their problems. He had a word and a smile for everyone, inmates and staff alike. There was a quality about his approach that meant that whoever he spoke to immediately felt a little better.

His presence brought reassurance and a little of the outside world to men separated from family and friends and who no longer had the familiar trappings of family life. He was known to be very good with young prisoners and those newly committed, always ready to give support and a sympathetic listening ear to those who needed it. He took Sunday services not only in the chapel but arranged informal services on the wings which he found to be more satisfactory than large gatherings in the chapel, where it was not unusual for inmates to use the occasion for plotting all kinds of schemes to upset the regime.

Robert gave of his time most willingly and would see anybody privately who made a request. His ministry extended outside the walls because he often visited prisoners' families at home when a relationship was in danger of breaking down or when a relative was ill. His familiar, slight figure was always ready to take on board anybody's problems. He was totally dedicated to the prisoners, also to staff, uniformed or governor grades, and could be relied on to offer sound advice and sympathy.

⋆

Terrence Medway, chairman of the appointments panel, opened his folder in front of him, saying, 'Now, we come to the last applicant, Dr Angela Cooper. I see this lady is well qualified. She qualified six years ago, and as you can see she has been a house surgeon at St Mary's in London and she has spent a year in the General Hospital at High Wycombe, and since then she has been in general practice in that area. Her references are quite excellent. Shall we have her in? I see she is a widow and has a child of five. Very sad.'

The panel looked at Angela as she came in and the chairman invited her to be seated. They saw a slim young woman with short fair hair, a high, intelligent forehead, blue eyes and small features who gave an overall impression of confidence. Her clothes were simple but elegant. When she smiled she suddenly looked quite beautiful.

'Good afternoon, Dr Cooper. I would, on behalf of this panel and myself, offer you condolences on the death of your husband.'

'Thank you very much.'

'Now, I see from your CV that you are well qualified for this appointment with Drs Graham and Hanley who are with us today. I must ask you, why you have chosen to come up to Manchester?'

'Well, partly to make a fresh start after my husband's death and partly because coming up here would fit in with my domestic arrangements concerning my small son.'

'I see. Dr Cooper, you have been in general practice but there is one aspect of this appointment which it is unlikely that you will have come across before: that is that this practice takes on the responsibility, with another practice, to look after the inmates of a large prison. Have you considered what working in a large prison entails?'

'Well, yes, I have thought about this. Of course, I have no personal experience of prisons. I hope I will be able to cope; prisoners are, after all, patients to be cared for. Also, the responsibility will be shared with other doctors and it is not as if I would be in the prison all the time.'

'Well, I think I must point out to you that you will come across some very awkward characters and some unpleasant cases, for example, suicides and attempted suicides. Thank you for attending this interview. We will be in touch with you. In the meantime, before you come to any decision about accepting this appointment, I suggest you make an appointment to see round the prison and have a talk with Dr Manners, who is retiring but will, I am sure, be very helpful to you. Good day, Dr Cooper.'

'Thank you. I will do that.'

Dr Medway turned to his colleagues, 'Dr Cooper seems to be a very suitable applicant. I just wonder if she will be able to cope with the inmates of the prison.'

Angela, as advised, made an appointment with Dr Manners a few days later. Over a cup of coffee in his office, Dr Manners said, 'Well, Angela, I may call you Angela? A prison is no place for a pretty girl like you, even if you are a doctor. What can I tell you? To start at the beginning. This is a committal prison, that is, we take all and everyone straight from the courts. We can house as many as five hundred men from a wide range of backgrounds, including non-Christians, that is Jews, Rastafarians, Muslims, Hindus – you name it, we have it. This in itself causes problems, although conditions are now much better than they were say ten years ago; for example there is now one man to a cell where I can remember three men were squeezed in a cell hardly large enough to house one. They can wear their own clothes if they have them. Their earnings are increased.

They may rent TV for their cells. They have access to payphones and, best of all, the abominable system of slopping out is but a thing of the past. However, I have to say that prison is still prison and many of the old stresses and heartbreaks remain. Prison lore dies hard. From time to time prisoners are frustrated and then trouble starts. First they are merely uncooperative and use foul language. Next they become violent and turn on the staff or each other. Then they may go on the rampage, burning or breaking up anything to hand. This is when you may be called in to patch up and deal with the casualties. How does this strike you?'

Angela took a deep breath. She wanted very much to move to this area because her aunt had offered to housekeep for her and, more importantly, she was a kindly person who would look after Ian when she was working and he was not at school. 'I hope I can cope.'

'Well, perhaps you can. I wish you luck. I am not sorry to be leaving. After a time it becomes all too much. After all I have said to put you off, I will add that the prison orderlies in the hospital are first-class and very helpful. They know the ropes and have seen it all before. Goodbye to you, Angela, and good luck.'

Angela took up the appointment with the practice some weeks later and with that the duties as part-time medical officer to the prison. She did not find her work there too distressing or unduly arduous. As Dr Manners had said, the hospital staff were both efficient and co-operative. Mr Grant, the senior orderly, was a fully-trained mental nurse with many years' experience. Usually he could tell Angela which of the inmates who came to see her were likely to be genuinely ill and who might be malingering. Angela, however, knew she must always be extremely careful not to miss anything.

It was several months before she met Robert.

Chapter Twenty-One

One day Robert found he was presented with a problem about which he felt he needed to consult with the MO before he could give any advice. He made his way to the hospital where he hoped to see the doctor. On this occasion Angela was on duty.

Robert knocked on the office door and on entering he proceeded to begin to explain his mission when quite suddenly everything went black and he passed out.

When he came round, two orderlies had removed him to an examination couch. He quickly recovered, feeling foolish. Angela asked him a little about himself and also if, by any chance, he had had any lunch. He then remembered that he had altogether forgotten to have any. Angela strongly recommended that he should go home and rest for the remainder of the day.

When he had gone, Mr Grant said, 'You know, Doctor, it is hardly surprising that the Padre passed out. He pushes himself very hard. He is supposed to be chaplain to the Anglican prisoners but he is a friend to everybody here and gives of his time to anyone with a problem and believe me, Doctor, they don't half unburden themselves to him. He never seems to mind. It is strange, even the worst of them behave like lambs when he is about. Am I saying too much, Doctor?'

'No, not at all.'

'Oh well, there is not really much more to say. Padre Robert, as he is known all over the establishment, is a decent sort; more than that, he is a perfect gentleman. I wish I had his dedication.'

On the following day, when doing his rounds and feeling none the worse, he met Angela again. 'How are you feeling today?'

'I am absolutely fine, thank you.'

After that he quite often dropped in on the hospital, and if Angela was there they had morning coffee together. During one of these sessions she told him, 'I am a widow. My husband died of leukaemia just over a year ago.'

Robert said, 'I am so sorry. I did not know. He paused. 'I was much luckier.'

'What do you mean "luckier"?'

Robert seldom spoke about himself and found it difficult but having gone so far he thought he had better explain.

'I had leukaemia when I was about ten, but I made a remarkable recovery, I am told, partly because I had a bone marrow transplant. My father donated bone marrow and I recovered, but sadly he died not long after the operation to extract it. Apparently it is most unusual for a donor to die. He was so unlucky and I have always been fortunate in my life.'

Angela sighed, 'Graham's leukaemia was a very acute form. He died not long after he was diagnosed. He had just started his chemotherapy. At least he was spared a long illness. He would have found that difficult to bear. He was thirty-three years old, such a vital person. We have a son called Ian who is now nearly five and hardly remembers his father, which is sad for him.' Then Angela added, 'Would you like to meet Ian? What do you do in your free time? I am told you put in a great deal of time here, far more than the other chaplains.'

'Well, perhaps I do, but I do not have any family near by. My people come from the north-west of Ireland. I go over there twice a year because my adopted parents are quite elderly. I also have a half-sister in London. We are very close.'

'Well, what about coming to have supper with us next Sunday?'

'I would like that very much.'

Robert visited a large bookshop and enlisted the help of a shop assistant to help him choose some books suitable for a five year old. Armed with these, and some flowers for Angela, Robert felt elated about the prospect of spending an evening with the two of them.

The evening passed off quite well, Angela asking Robert, 'What do you do for relaxation and recreation?'

Robert thought before answering, 'I like to go walking when I have time. I watch a lot of football on the television, not because I really like it but because it is a most useful topic of conversation, one which really draws the lads out.'

Angela followed this by asking, 'What do you do about meals?' rightly guessing that he did not look after himself properly.

'I usually lunch in the staff canteen and that takes care of my main meal and, more importantly, gives me a good opportunity to get to know the staff.'

Angela knew that their friendship was developing into something more. She found she was drawn to Robert who was so unlike Graham – Graham who had done everything at top speed, proposing to her within weeks of meeting her in the hospital where they both worked and marrying her within three months of their first meeting. He was passionate in his lovemaking, ever talkative and argumentative, quick-tempered but generous to a degree. She had loved him and she missed him, but he had not been an easy person to live with.

Graham always had to be the centre of attention wherever he was and he rarely listened to what other people were saying, especially not to Angela. Even his dying had been sudden and dramatic, leaving Angela saddened but exhausted and drained.

Robert was everything Graham was not. He was gentle and calm, a quiet person, even-tempered and always thought before he spoke. His voice was another thing, a very slight accent with a wonderful velvet-like quality which attracted listeners to absorb every single word. All were very carefully chosen; never was any word superfluous.

His appearance may not be very striking, unlike the handsome Graham, but when he spoke he was impressive. Angela felt comfortable in his company. She was sure he would be an easy person to live with.

Yes, she thought. I will marry him when he asks me. She thought that it would not be 'if' but 'when' he asked her.

Robert continued to have supper with Angela on Sundays and sometimes during the week. After Ian was in bed they enjoyed long discussions about books they had read or could recommend to each other, or about journeys they had made or cities they had visited, or about art. They touched on topical matters such as the question of women priests and celibacy in the Roman Catholic Church, or they merely relaxed and listened to music if Robert felt very tired, which was quite often the case.

Robert was reluctant to talk about himself or how he felt and he made no advances to her. Yet Angela was sure he did have deeper feelings for her. Eventually she decided to ask him a little about himself.

'Tell me, Robert,' she said one evening as they were enjoying a cup of coffee. 'You say your father is dead. What about your mother?'

'I really know very little about her. I believe she is in Perth, Australia. She disappeared when I was a few weeks old. I don't know why. I have no feelings about her. I wish her well, but I don't really want to see or get in touch with her. I was fostered when I was four years old and I had the most wonderful foster parents. They are now very old. I do visit them at least twice a year and keep in touch by telephone, as they do not now feel up to making the journey over here. They have two married daughters and almost grown-up grandchildren. They are a close family and I was so fortunate to become one of them. Never a day passes that I do not thank God that these good people took me into their care when my mother left me in a children's home. My mother and father were not married.'

He paused and looked almost as if he could not continue. 'Don't tell me if you'd rather not, if it is painful for you. It is just that I have grown to care a great deal about you and I am genuinely interested. I think you care for me. Am I not right?' said Angela.

'I think perhaps I would like to tell you that my father was in prison serving a long sentence for a terrorist offence. I do not think he was the usual type of terrorist, but rather a weak character who was sucked into an illegal organisation and was caught red-handed. It is a complicated and sad story. He did not know about me until after he was in prison and had been for some considerable time and he heard it on the grapevine quite by chance. He contacted the Robinsons, that is my foster parents, for whom he had once worked. He told them that his son was in a children's home, that he himself had been an orphan and had spent most of his childhood in care and he just did not want that for me. He begged them to find suitable foster parents for me and they ended up taking me into their family. I believe he always hoped they would do this. They were not very young even then but they are wonderful Christian people. I cannot tell you how much I love and how much I owe them. No boy could have had a happier childhood than I did. For a long time I thought my father was dead, and although they visited him in prison and even invited him to spend Christmas Day with the family when he had leave, we thought it was just one of their acts of Christian charity, that is, asking a prisoner for Christmas. That was the first time I saw my father, though I did not know who he was at that time. They thought that was best. At first when he arrived he was very shy and awkward, but we children, that is the other grandchildren and myself, in our excitement over Christmas soon were chatting away to him. He brought us presents. For me there was a painting of the family dog, a black Labrador called Folly and much loved by me. I suppose Da and Lou, which is what I called my foster parents, had told him about our dog on one of their visits to Magilligan. I expect it must have been difficult to keep the conversation flowing. In many ways they were poles apart. My father was an uneducated farm labourer and they were very cultured people. I would have been the common denominator. Anyhow, my father was an artist, as it turned out later, of considerable talent. I was delighted with the picture and it still hangs in my room in their house. That Christmas he promised to paint pictures for the other children of a pony and of a tractor for the smallest little boy. I don't know if he ever did these or not. Am I boring you? I did not see my father again until I was in hospital and even then I did not really know who he was. I was feeling pretty ill and muddled and confused. I think I was just told he was the kind donor of bone marrow which could help to make me better. They did not tell me for some time that he had died. A nurse told me donors were usually close relatives and so I thought maybe he was my brother. Much later I asked if this was so and then Edward told me the whole story.'

Here Angela interrupted, 'Robert, was your father Michael Duffy, the artist whose work is associated with leukaemia research?'

'Yes, he was my natural father. His paintings made a great deal of money. A percentage went to medical research and the rest was put into trust for me. I am by no means poor. I do not have money worries. I am able, with the other members of the family, to contribute to paying for a really good housekeeper to take care of Lou and Edward in their own home for as long as they want to stay there. It is the very least I can do. They were so wise in their handling of me when I was growing up. In my late teens I realised that it was shameful to have a father who was in prison. I did have doubts and worries. Edward would say, "No need to publicise the fact. Fortunately, you have a different name and you should never be confronted with the truth. Just say your father made a bad and mistaken judgement, like many young men of his time, and he paid the price. Then you might add his last act was a most noble one." Then Louise, always so charitable, would say, "Tell them he was a young man who was unloved and disadvantaged with none of the advantages you have. He was capable of great love and he gave his life to save yours." Or again she would say he was a very great artist whose work, even after his death, contributes to medical research. Actually, I was rarely ever put in that position but their wisdom well prepared me for any difficulties which might have arisen and did worry me while I was still at school, even though I always had the security at home to shield me from untoward hurt. It was rather different when I went to Cambridge. Although nothing was ever said to me, I realised that I was different from most of the other undergraduates I met. I became more aware of my background and, whereas at home I could see my father as my benefactor and I overlooked the fact that he was a convicted terrorist, without my foster parents' backing I felt vulnerable and afraid of facing up to the truth. So I never confided in anyone and kept myself very much to myself. I am sure, now, that I was wrong about this, but I felt none of them would understand.'

Angela listened very carefully and said, when he had finished, 'You had remarkable foster parents. It must have been difficult for them too. That you had doubts about handling your situation when away from the security they gave you, when you went up to Cambridge, merely shows how wise they were. Did you finally come to terms with it and realise that nowadays people take you for what you are yourself and don't care one jot about who your parents were?'

'Well, yes. In time, as you say, I did come to terms with that side of my life; I realised I was indulging in self-pity. That was when I decided to go into the Church and I hoped to put something back into life, when I had been so fortunate in my own life. Once I had made that decision, things became clearer and I knew where I was going.'

'You mean to say that at that time you decided to become a prison chaplain and that is why you spend all the hours that God gives you in the prison? I will tell you quite bluntly, I don't think your father gave up his life for you to spend it almost entirely ministering to prisoners. I think he would have wanted you to have a normal life with a proper home, a life he never had. Robert, I am very fond of you and I hope you are fond of me and you will consider what I have said and start to live a little.'

Robert after a long pause said, 'Angela, does this mean that what I have just told you does not put you off me, or, to be more explicit, it would not be an impediment to us having a more permanent relationship? I should have given you more credit than to have thought you were a small-minded person, not that this is a small matter. Many good people would not consider me under any circumstances.'

'Well, maybe, but not for those reasons, Robert.'

'Angela, will you marry me? I cannot believe that I have once again in my life been so very fortunate as to have a chance of such happiness. Marry me and soon, please, Angela.'

'Robert, I solemnly will consider your proposal, if you can promise to change a little. You must put the past behind you and I could help you if you will. Forgive me for saying this but I see you as almost a saint. Saints are all very well but a trifle boring and certainly I would not be married to one. Now, I am not asking you to become a great sinner, but just a little more human. Keep those prisoners where they belong and give them your good offices but you will have to consider me and Ian, not necessarily before them, but certainly as well and as important to you. Can you do this? If you can, the answer is yes – I will be happy to marry you.'

Robert and Angela were married three weeks later by special licence.

Chapter Twenty-Two

Anne made a telephone call to her sister in County Wicklow. 'Hello, Mary. I have some news for you. Robert was married last weekend to a lady doctor, a widow with a small son.'

'This is indeed good news. I think he led an awful life, spending all his time in that prison. Do Mum and Dad know yet? I am sure they will be pleased.'

'I have a suggestion to make to you. You remember it is Dad's eightieth birthday quite soon. Why don't we arrange a bumper party for him and get all the family together so that they could meet Robert's new wife and son?'

'What a good idea.'

'I was thinking of instead of us all going to the house in Derry, we should go to a hotel in Donegal for a long weekend. Frankly, I think this would be more attractive for the younger folk.'

Several days later Anne again rang Mary. 'Robert has telephoned Mum and Dad and told them he was married, and they immediately said they would like to meet Angela and her son Ian. So that will fit well with my idea of a party for dad. Now I have found what I think may be the best possible venue for this party cum reunion. I have been told that there are the most super chalets on Lough Erne. They are very well appointed with every possible comfort, in fact quite luxurious in the most lovely surroundings. Mum and Dad might enjoy this more than a hotel. The bonus is that the package comes with a boat with an outboard motor and there is an adjacent golf course and heaps of things for the active members of the clan to do and you know that is important. Do you think we should seriously consider this?'

'Why yes! It sounds an excellent idea, Anne. You are always full of good ideas.'

'Well, I have checked Dad's birthday and it is 25th May, which takes in the Whit weekend. If you like, I will fly over to Enniskillen and look over these chalets and if they are all that I have been told they were I shall make the necessary arrangements.'

Robert, Angela and Ian travelled to Ireland by Seacat. They picked up a hire car and drove to County Fermanagh to join the Robinsons' family party.

Edward, in spite of his eighty years, was sprightly and as hale as ever. Louise, a few years younger, also enjoyed good health despite suffering from a degree of deafness and some arthritis. Both were looking forward to having their family together. Anne had made all the arrangements.

Edward thought, Anne is so capable and so thoughtful. This is certainly a beautiful place. I never knew Fermanagh was a place of such outstanding natural beauty – a perfect setting for this celebration.

Louise and Edward were dozing on the veranda in the evening sunshine, awaiting the arrival of the family and the commencement of the party. Louise opened her eyes and she saw a small boy looking up at her. For a moment she was quite confused and thought it was Robert.

She turned and said to Edward, 'How nice that Robert is here today!' Then she quickly realised her mistake and said, 'What is your name and how old are you?'

'My name is Ian and I am five and a half. I have a new father and he is going to take me out in a boat on that lake you can see over there and we are going to fish.'

Now Robert came and kissed Louise and Edward and, smiling, said, 'Lou, Edward, let me introduce you to my wife, Angela. You have already met Ian.'

Before they sat down to dinner Anne called on Robert to say grace.

'Benedicite. Bless us Oh Lord, and this family which I am fortunate to belong to. Bless especially Edward and Louise, and we give you thanks for all the blessings we have received through their goodness. Amen.'

The meal then commenced amid cheerful chatter. Anne had done them proud. Before the coffee, Anne, as prime mover, was asked to propose a toast.

Raising her glass, she said in a clear voice, 'I propose a toast to Edward and Louise, our much-loved parents, grand parents and foster parents. To all of us they are very special. We wish Edward many happy returns on his eightieth birthday. Today we are happy to welcome into our family Angela and Ian, and I hope we will see them very often.'

Edward rose to his feet and said, 'Louise and I thank you all for the superb party, for your kind words, good wishes and unfailing love. I cannot remember an occasion we have enjoyed more than this. Once again, thank you all. Louise and I are a little tired and now I think we will retire.'

Angela whispered to Robert, 'I think Ian is almost asleep. I think we had better take him back to the farmhouse to bed. I will just say goodnight to Louise and Edward quietly – we don't want to break up a good party.'

Robert went over and kissed both Louise and Edward. Softly, Louise said into his ear, 'Robert, we are so happy for you. Angela is a very nice person and seems so right for you. I am sure poor Michael Duffy could not have wished anything more for you.'

With that Robert and Angela, and a very sleepy Ian, slipped away.

Chapter Twenty-Three

After five years of a happy marriage, Angela began to notice a change in Robert. He was losing weight, sleeping badly and seemed to have lost his appetite. He was, at times, quite irritable with her and Ian, and this was quite out of character. She feared he might be ill and begged him to have a check-up.

Robert assured her he was not ill, but he did confess, 'For some reason my work in the prison is not going well. Previously I could always cope, and even derived a certain degree of job satisfaction. Now it is becoming a burden. I lie awake at night wondering why it is that I am failing to help the men. I sympathise with them but I just can't offer any help or support to them. I know I should not bring my worries home to you.'

When Robert had seen doctors and undergone tests, they could not find anything physically wrong with him.

Angela decided that the time had come for Robert to change his lifestyle and job if necessary. As a first step, she studied the medical journals until she found several general practices that were looking for an assistant with a view to becoming a partner – one in Devon and one in Cambridge. The latter immediately appealed to her. If they could go to Cambridge, Ian could go to any one of the excellent schools and surely there would be something for Robert, and wouldn't Cambridge be a more attractive place to live than Manchester, although she had to admit they were quite happy there.

Without telling Robert exactly what she was about to do, she travelled to Cambridge, leaving her aunt in charge, and only when she was fairly sure that this job could be hers if she wanted it did she make enquiries as to what kind of positions might be available for Robert. She was relieved to learn there might be several openings in the area, either in parishes or as a team minister undertaking work in several parishes, as there were apparently not nearly enough priests to minister to all the churches in the dioceses. In fact, she learnt there was a great shortage of ministers overall.

So, tentatively, she approached Robert on her return, knowing this was not going to be easy. 'Robert, we must talk. I know something is troubling you. We must get to the bottom of it. Thank God you are not ill, as I feared. What then?'

'No, I am not sick but I am burnt out as regards my ministry in the prison. I don't know why but I can no longer deal with the men. I feel a complete failure. By and large, they are no different but I can no longer take on board their troubles, however hard I try, and what is worst, I seem to have lost interest and most certainly I have now very little patience with them. I used to think I had a vocation to help prisoners. Now I have grave doubts. Oh, Angela, what am I to do?'

'I have known for some time that all was not well with you. I think you need a change of scene. Have you thought about different work? The prison is suffocating you – after all, you have been there a very long time.'

Angela remembered what Dr Manners had said to her about the prison work becoming all too much after a long time and she thought this must apply to ministers as well as doctors. She realised she must press on at this point if she was going to persuade Robert to see things as she did.

'Robert, I hate to say this, but if you don't snap out of this slough of depression you are going to damage and even destroy our marriage and hurt Ian, who really loves you.'

Robert was distressed and even shocked to think he was likely to cause pain to Angela and Ian. Angela was also troubled. She knew Robert was a genuinely sincere person and she did not want to knock him when he was in low spirits, but she also felt she must be blunt if Robert was to consider giving up his prison ministry. She honestly felt he needed a change, so she continued. 'I think you will have to choose between Ian and me and those men in prison. There is not room in your life for both.'

Robert would have been reluctant to admit it, but he felt a flood of relief at the thought of not having to continue in the prison. He felt grateful to Angela for making a decision that he would never have made himself.

Angela, seeing that she had made her point with Robert, proceeded to lead him to consider her plans for their future. 'I have been making enquiries about jobs for both of us. I am told there are many openings in the rural areas in the diocese of Cambridge and I can get a job there if I want. I would very much like to move there. Cambridge is such a civilised place; you would appreciate being there, I know, and I would like Ian to try for a place at St John's. This is the right time for him to change schools.'

Robert saw his bishop, who was very understanding, and agreed that Robert was in need of a change. 'Your wife is right. If you are finding the prison ministry a burden, you certainly won't be of much use to the men there. I know you have personal reasons for undertaking this work but I would say you have fulfilled your obligations in that direction, and there are many ways to serve; there are many others in need as well as those unfortunate men behind bars – remember that. I will do what I can to find a suitable vacancy for you in the Cambridge area. It will most likely be in a rural region – that is where there is a great scarcity of clergy. Goodbye and God bless you, Robert.'

At the end of that year Robert, Angela, Ian and Aunt Maud, who at the last moment decided she was part of the family and did not want to be parted from them and Ian in particular, all left Manchester, not without some misgivings on Robert's part. They rented a cottage in Clare and Ian started school at St John's, where he settled down well.

Robert almost immediately became a member of a team of ministers covering numerous churches. The congregations were very small, and at first Robert thought there would be very little to do, but he soon discovered that because there was no regular priest, many elderly and housebound people were seldom visited. Mothers' Union and youth groups and even Sunday school had fallen into abeyance. He set to and tried to address these and many other shortcomings. Soon he became well known and much in demand. He was always busy, but he experienced no stress.

He was delighted when he was offered a lectureship in Theology at the college from which he had graduated many years ago. This was a challenge but soon became a source of joy and inspiration. In order to teach he had to return to his books and study. He had forgotten the magic that was Cambridge; the contact with undergraduates, their youth and enthusiasm enriched his life. He realised and was constantly grateful to Angela whose wisdom had saved him from a course which most certainly would have led to disaster for him, when he was too short-sighted and proud to see what was happening to him.

But Robert soon found himself on the horns of a dilemma. His reputation from Manchester caught up with him as he was offered an appointment as relief chaplain at Highpoint Prison, with a view to becoming part-time Anglican chaplain to replace the retiring chaplain. Did this mean he was meant to be a part of prison life? Was this a second chance to fulfil his vocation? He just did not know. He realised how much he depended on Angela, as he turned to her for advice.

'Accept if you must, by all means, but remember that you are a priest, a husband and a father. If you can combine these roles with prison visiting, so be it; but never let it take over.'

Postscript

Elsie looked at her daughter and wished she could persuade her to leave well alone and not rake up the past which she would rather not remember. She did not want her to go all the way to England or Ireland to visit her brother, but she knew that once Sarah had set her heart on something, nothing would deter her. Why did Elsie feel so strongly that visiting Robert would be a mistake? Was it because she still felt guilty that she had deserted him all those years ago? No, it was not that, because she had been assured that Robert was in a very good home, and more than that, he was very much loved and he had become part of a well-to-do family. He was being brought up to be a gentleman. The solicitors had recommended that she should not take him away from people that had taken him and made him part of their family. She could never have hoped to give him such a start in life. True, she had very readily agreed to this, but she told herself that had she not had such favourable reports about the Robinson family, she would have sent for the child or even fetched him. Bill, her husband, would not have objected.

Perhaps she did feel a little guilty and did not want to be reminded of Robert, but she could not say she felt anything other than this guilt. She recalled that she had not wanted a child at that time, and that when he was born she just could not take to him, let alone love him, and if she remembered rightly, the baby had been positively hostile to her, an angry, screaming infant. She just did not want Sarah to get mixed up with the Robinsons and Robert, who was now a grown man. How was it that Sarah wanted to know a brother she had never seen in all her twenty-three years? It was all this modern theory they taught nurses nowadays. Oh well, perhaps they would not want to meet Sarah.

Sarah, as her mother rightly assumed, was not easily put off once she had made her mind up about something. When, some years ago, Elsie had casually mentioned that she had had a son many years ago, when she had lived in Ireland before she had married Sarah's father, Sarah had immediately wanted to know about her brother, and bit by bit she had extracted everything that Elsie could tell her. How could she have done such a thing?

Elsie had tried to explain that the child had been left in the care of a good and decent man and that she had only finally given up all claim to him when she heard that her former husband had been killed and that Robert was being brought up by well-to-do folk, as one of their family. Had it not been so, Elsie told her daughter, and had she had not been assured that it would be very much in the boy's best interest to be left with that family, she would have fetched him and brought him out to Perth.

'Your father would have accepted him.'

Sarah said nothing, but she made up her mind that as soon as it was possible she would travel to England or Ireland and find her brother. He might not want to know her, but she wanted to know him. After all, he was her brother.

She did not mention any of this again to Elsie until she had completed her nursing training. Elsie had conveniently put the matter out of her mind. She had always been able to do this regarding anything she found disturbing or unpleasant.

'Ma,' said Sarah, when visiting the family home adjacent to her father's general store and garage, 'I am going to

England for a year. I can now get a temporary nursing position almost anywhere as I am fully trained. I am quite excited about it. Wish me luck. I will keep you and Dad fully posted of all I do and see there.'

Sarah did not tell her mother that she had been to the solicitors in Swan Street and asked them to trace her mother's son, Robert. She had not known his surname and she was surprised and pleased when, after several weeks, they were not only able to tell her his name but also that he was married, living in Cambridge and also that he was an Anglican priest. The solicitors told her that they had contacted the Robinsons' solicitors in Londonderry, Northern Ireland, and that they had been willing to provide Robert's half-sister with these detail, and that they had said furthermore that they would inform Robert that his sister would be contacting him. Sarah was surprised and amazed that it should have been so easy to trace Robert.

So Sarah travelled to Britain. She was excited at the thought of seeing England and of seeing all the famous places in London, familiar to her from picture books she remembered from when she was a small girl. The thought of finding her brother was uppermost in her mind above all else. Other girls she was at school with, and the girls who had been through the nursing training with her, all seemed to have brothers, sisters, cousins, uncles, aunts, grannies and grandfathers, and she only had a mother and father. True, she did love them and knew they loved her, but she always thought it would be fun to have a family.

It had been very difficult to extract information about her brother, but she had persisted and here she was, touching down at Heathrow, England. She had made her plans carefully as to how she would proceed. She had the name and address of a nursing agency through which she would be able to find employment. She knew this was important because her savings would not last very long.

As she left the aircraft, all her fellow passengers appeared to know exactly where to go. A little unsure, she followed them, claimed her two pieces of luggage and made her way to an information desk, hoping the official there would direct her on her way into London. As it turned out, this person was extremely helpful and advised her to take the Underground and then a taxi to the agency, adding that there was a YMCA hostel within walking distance.

At the agency, Sarah handed in her certificates and letters of recommendation from the hospital in Perth where she had completed her training and also worked as a staff nurse for a year in surgical and medical wards. Sarah was suddenly overcome with fatigue and a degree of homesickness. A computer showed that, had she been willing, she could have gone on night duty that very evening, but it was quite obvious that she was suffering from jet lag and was advised to check in at the hostel and report the following evening. It was explained to Sarah that she could expect to be engaged for night duty but would be unlikely to get daytime duties, and that she would be expected to fill in at various hospitals.

She checked in at the hostel and almost immediately fell into bed and slept soundly for nearly twelve hours. It was only after breakfast that she was able to take any real notice of her surroundings. She looked out onto the rather dismal street and decided to take a bus into the West End.

On the leaving the bus she realised how cold and damp it was, how crowded the streets were. Everybody seemed to be in a terrific hurry.

She found her way to Buckingham Palace and stood at the railings, wondering if the Queen was in residence. In spite of many other sightseers she felt strange and rather lonely. Nobody took the slightest notice of her, and for the first time she wondered if she had been wise to come all this way to find a brother who, for all she knew, might not want to know her.

Still tired after the long flight, more and more doubts filled her mind. Would she be able to cope with nursing here in London? Would she ever get used to the cold? Should she consider going home again? Had her mother been right – was it a mistake to rake up the past?

Sarah need not have worried about nursing in London. As advised by the agency, she reported to St Mark's Hospital and was immediately directed to the ward she was to work on. The day and night staff were just changing over. She was politely greeted and given a report on the patients who would be in her care for the night. She found she just slotted in as though she was in the hospital in Perth. The patients accepted her administrations exactly as patients always had, and she did her best to make them comfortable. She found the other nurses and nursing assistants friendly and helpful.

By morning, although tired, she was greatly reassured to find that the routine was much the same as she was accustomed to. She worked in the same hospital for a week and then was sent to another, by which time she had regained her confidence and was settling down. She became friendly with a Canadian nurse, also staying at the hostel and working on night duty. They went sightseeing together and exchanged their views on all they saw.

Sarah decided she was very disappointed with London; she could not get used to the crowds everywhere, nor to the cold which made her buy some extra warm pullovers. Barbara, on the other hand, loved the cut and thrust that was London. Sarah decided it was time to contact Robert and she wrote a carefully worded letter, asking if he would meet her in Cambridge if she went down there. The agency had a branch in Cambridge and gave Sarah a letter of introduction.

Barbara announced that she would go to Cambridge with her and, if she liked, would share a flat with her for a month or so. Together they took the bus to Cambridge. Sarah fell in love with Cambridge on sight and was charmed with all she saw. Even Barbara was impressed.

They were fortunate to find a flat to rent, a very small flat at the top of an old-fashioned house. From their windows they could see a lovely stretch of green and the river and King's College. Sarah found it delightful.

Barbara, although quite pleased, said, 'I could do with a few more mod cons and less view. However, it will do.'

They both got appointments, Barbara at Addenbrookes and Sarah at a private hospital. She was pleased to find that they would take her on for a month with a view to a permanent appointment if she proved to be satisfactory. Also, she would only be required to do night duty every other week. Sarah loved this hospital and also Cambridge. She bought a second-hand bicycle and cycled in to the little hospital every day, well wrapped up against the icy winds which seemed to blow most of the time.

When they had been in Cambridge for two weeks, a letter arrived for Sarah from Robert, giving his telephone number and inviting her to telephone him and make an arrangement to visit.

When Robert first heard from the solicitors in Londonderry that his half-sister was about to contact him, his first reaction was one of complete surprise. Long ago he had ceased to think about his natural mother. He bore her no ill will; she just meant nothing to him. If he was to be honest with himself, having a sister did not, at first, mean very much either, but as he thought more about it he realised that, 'As a Christian, which I aspire to be, I must make her welcome.'

Turning to Angela, he added, 'I know you will go along with this and give me your support. There is a part of me, of which I am not very proud, that asks what this girl wants? Why does she suddenly make herself known to me after all this time?'

Angela replied, 'Perhaps you should be asking yourself what Sarah, that is her name, needs?'

'Of course, you are absolutely right. I just hope that I can meet her needs.'

'Everybody has something of themselves to give to others, and, if I know you, you have more than most. Just be yourself and she will love you.'

'Well, I hope so. We will soon know.'

Another letter arrived for Robert saying, if convenient, Sarah would like to come to see Robert and his family on the following Saturday, which would be her next free day.

Sarah enjoyed the bus ride from Cambridge and she was enchanted when she reached Clare. She thought, This is just how I always imagined England to be like – so quaint and so pretty.

She enquired at the post office cum general store as to how she would find 'Berries', the home of the Reverend Draper.

She was directed to the outskirts of the village. As she made her way, doubts came flooding back and her confidence ebbed away. By the time she reached the lovely honey-coloured house in its lilac-scented garden of flowering shrubs and many flowers, she said to herself, 'I feel I am a nervous wreck. How should I proceed? Should I proceed at all? Do I look all right? I wonder if Robert will like the paperweight? I hope so. It cost me quite a bit, but I thought it was lovely. The alexandrite chippings are so polished and change colour in different lights. It should look very nice on his desk. No one will know what it is and he will say, "My sister brought me this from Australia". Will his little boy like the boomerang? Will his doctor wife like the chocolates? I just hope she is not one of those ladies always dieting and, oh dear, will they disapprove of me because my voice is different from the way they speak?'

Sarah forced herself forward and gently knocked on the door. A minute passed and then she was facing Robert. Her first impression was of a very slight man, hardly any taller than she was, but he looked kind as he said, 'You must be Sarah. Come in. I am Robert.'

Sarah shyly went forward. Clutching her parcels in one hand, she held out the other to take Robert's outstretched hand. Words failed her. She felt almost choked with emotion as she smiled at her brother.

'You have come a long way to find us, Sarah, and we are delighted to have you with us.' This was what Robert had prepared to say to his sister. As he took her hand in his, suddenly he knew he really meant every word of it. The contact with his sister, who had travelled across the globe to find him, became a precious reality. He became aware of the sweetness of her person.

He took her in his arms and hugged her and silently he offered a prayer of thanksgiving, then called out, 'Angela! Ian! Come and meet Sarah, who has just come to join our family.'